A SIBLI

BUTTERFLY

CHRISTOPHER THOMPSON

Cover image by: Kerry Ellis
Book design by: SWATT Books Ltd

Printed in the United Kingdom
First Printing, 2023

ISBN: 979-8-9885274-0-4 (Paperback)
ISBN: 979-8-9885274-1-1 (eBook)

Christopher Thompson
Menlo Park, California

This book is dedicated to Chayton, Chenoa, Jo,
and the butterflies that watch over them.

CONTENTS

PROLOGUE

PIGS

CHAYTON WALKED BEHIND his dad as they exited the stone-paved driveway and made their way up the narrow, bamboo-strewn path that led to their neighbor's compound. Since his Indonesian was better than his dad's—who would debate that his Indonesian wasn't *terrible*—he tagged along to discuss relocating their neighbor's pig farm.

Pig farms didn't make for good neighborly company. The foul smell and the nonstop noise made everyone lose their minds, particularly Chayton's mom. She also loved animals and knew those pigs' fates.

"Wouldn't it be cool to go back in time and see what Bali was like without so many people?" his dad asked.

"Um. Maybe," the tall boy responded as he flung his matted curly blond hair away from his face.

The tropical air often felt devoid of oxygen, thick and humid. The relentless heat clung their clothes to their sticky skin. Their breathing was labored. Cicadas' shrill, relentless wine whipped through the dense forest. It was midday yet only sparse sunrays broke through the tree canopy.

Chayton wanted to be watching *Ozark* on Netflix at home, not walking and theorizing in the heat. And particularly not talking about pigs. Lots of philosophizing occurred these days as the world was stuck in lockdown. Shut people inside, and their minds will spin.

"What if all the people in the world were just gone?" his dad continued. "I know this sounds kind of sucky, but consider how there were only a billion people in the world just over a hundred years ago. Now we have eight billion. That's just too many people causing too much damage. Imagine Bali with just a handful of people swimming in pristine oceans with vibrant coral reefs. Amazing!"

"Yeah. That would be kind of cool, Dad. Maybe not *amazing*," he responded, emphasizing the word his dad used too often. Everything was *amazing* to his father. "Maybe just fewer people would be better. I'm not sure getting rid of *everyone* is a good idea. That may be a bit too Thanos-like, snapping your fingers and half the world just disappears. But I get your point."

"You're probably right, son. Just a thought."

A shrill scream ripped through the forest from the compound ahead. Their neighbors were slaughtering a pig for the Galungan ceremony that evening to welcome the ancestral spirits back to Earth.

Chayton looked up and shuddered.

"Come on, Chay," his dad said. "Let's get this over with."

Another cry came.

He remembered how pigs could sense death.

CHAPTER 1

HERONS

THE VALLEY WAS still.

To the east, a flock of herons crested the ridge, flying over two huddled children on a porch. The long Ayung River rushed through the forested ravine below. Its strong rapids pushed by all the rocks and the land, not seeming to notice the children. They sat together with their knees touching, closer than usual for teen siblings.

"I miss them, Chayton," Chenoa whispered.

"Me too, Chenoa," he responded as he stared at the ravine. "Me too."

"Do you think they are okay?" she asked, not really wanting an answer.

The boy remained silent.

Their parents had flown to Australia for their dad to compete in the Perth to Rottnest twenty-kilometer swim, famous for the fact that sharks swam below the swimmers during the race. No one in the family understood why anyone would want to swim that far and with sharks. But their dad loved swimming and swam in their pool every day. Ever since he was little, he loved the water, being a Pisces and all. He had said that the water transported him to another world, and he could forget the day's pains and distractions there.

The parents had left a week prior to have some time together before the competition. Chayton and Chenoa hadn't heard from them since.

They hadn't heard from anyone since.

A week ago, they were watching a movie in the media room when the house rocked. Earthquakes were common in Bali, but this was different. Something violently pounded on the house, shaking the windows and the sliding glass doors. They jumped up to the window and looked out toward the morning sun. A cloud of smoke darkened the sky, and the sun disappeared.

"Chayton...?" Chenoa muttered, twisting the bracelets on her wrists.

They grabbed their phones. Social media reported that Mt. Agung had erupted, and lava was flowing down its eastern wall. The active volcano had erupted a few years prior, leading to the evacuation of 100,000 people within a twenty-kilometer radius around the mountain. Ash had billowed into the sky and rained down on the surrounding area. They remembered seeing the cloud spew from the volcano's mouth, a discernible funnel that spanned out to the south like an inverted tornado.

But this pyroclastic cloud rapidly expanded in all directions and was rolling toward them.

"Chenoa, shut the fucking doors!" Chayton screamed.

They sprinted through the house and shut all the doors and windows. As the light disappeared, an obscure memory came to Chayton. He recalled his dad wanting the house to close completely, unlike most local planned homes that had more openings. While his dad had said it was to get from one end of the house to the other during heavy rain, it probably had more to do with his ceaseless desire to keep everything clean.

All right, Dad. Let's see how clean this keeps things, he thought.

They both ran into Chayton's room, stumbled over the dirty clothes that littered the floor, closed the door, and huddled on his bed. They tried calling their parents, but all the lines were jammed.

YouTube videos showed reports of volcanic eruptions around the world: Russia, Italy, The United States, and New Zealand. Frantic reporters struggled to speak as dark clouds enveloped the air around them, and dust choked them.

"Chay, where is Kamchatka? The entire mountain just exploded," Chenoa said as she turned her phone in his direction.

He grabbed it from her and stared at the images on the screen. The volcano had blown outward, shooting lava and rocks everywhere. The video cut to a young girl screaming for her mother before a molten boulder wiped her from the shot.

These simultaneous violent eruptions darkened the skies around the entire world. Images showed people choking and twisted bodies stacking up in the streets.

Each image seemed to get more fearsome than the last. One after another.

Chayton shook his head and handed the phone back to her. "This can't be real, Chenoa. This must be fake. I mean, look at that! That's CGI. It can't be real."

It's real, she thought. She had studied volcanoes in school. Indonesia sat in the Ring of Fire, a horseshoe-shaped belt that was forty thousand kilometers in length. She had studied Krakatoa, one of the most violent volcanic eruptions in history that had completely destroyed its own island. Massive explosions had torn the volcano apart, producing tsunamis that devastated the region. The blast was thousands of times more powerful than the bomb that had destroyed Hiroshima. Ash from Krakatoa had circled the globe and dropped the world temperature by several degrees.

"We have reports of over five hundred volcanoes erupting around the world," a male news broadcaster reported as screams echoed in the background.

"Help us!" a woman shouted over him. "Help us!"

"Get the fuck away from me!" the reporter yelled as he pushed her to the ground.

The camera followed him as he ran into the melee.

Chayton and Chenoa repeatedly tried to contact their parents again, but the lines remained busy. Their electricity continued to work at least. And their overplanning parents had a commercial generator in case something else happened.

"We are here in Yosemite," a female broadcaster reported toward the camera, "and as you can see, steam is billowing from the mountain behind me. Experts and scientists have confirmed that Yosemite is safe and—"

The top of the mountain exploded, and the signal went dark.

Chayton and Chenoa's power went out a few hours later. The generator turned on as the world went dark. Lights from the villas and hotels across the valley gave out.

They fell asleep next to each other, clinging to their phones.

Dogs barking awoke Chayton and Chenoa the next morning. Kuma, their first rescue dog who was named after the Japanese word for bear because of her thick black fur, pawed at the outside door. They jumped out of bed and into darkness. The electricity was off since the generator had run out of diesel.

Chayton glanced at the clock and saw that it was just after ten a.m. He stumbled across the house and opened the door for Kuma. The sun tried to push through the murky skies, and a thin layer of ash covered the porch and lawn. He coughed and sneezed seven times, like he always did when he sneezed. The family used to think he was faking it until they realized it was out of his control.

"Bless you, Chayton," Chenoa said. "Are you feeling okay?"

"I guess so." He rubbed his sore throat. "No, not really."

Chenoa saw their rescue dog Machi, named after macchiato coffee for her brown and white coat, lying on her side and panting. Kubi, the black and smallest dog, was licking her face.

They had forgotten to bring the dogs in the night before.

Chenoa opened the doors and picked up the ash-covered Machi. She brought her inside, and the other dogs followed. Machi's breathing came in erratic pulses. Chenoa went into Chayton's room, set Machi beside him, and dribbled some water into her mouth. The dog lapped it with her tongue and lifted her head. She grabbed three bowls of dog food from the pantry and fed them in the bedroom.

When she came back, she realized Chayton hadn't moved an inch the whole time. He sat on the edge of the bed, holding his head. His face was paler than she had ever seen it before.

"You don't look so good, Chay," she admitted, grabbing a glass of water. "Here. Have some water."

"I'm not feeling so great," he said. "I need to lie down."

The usually punctual house staff had still not arrived for the day. She coughed and cleared her throat. Thinking something must've gotten in the air from when she let the dogs in, she searched for the N95 masks that her mom had bought to help people during Mt. Agung's last eruption. She put one on, grabbed one for Chayton, and went back to his room.

He was now lying on his bed and struggling to breathe. His breath was raspy and strained. She saw him lifting his head and shoulders to pull air into his lungs.

"Chay! Chay!" She wiped his face with some water and her shirt. She then put a glass to his lips. "Take a sip."

He sipped the water and coughed it out across the floor.

She held his head and spoke calmly. "Little sips, Chay. Just take little sips." In reality, she had no idea what she was doing, but she hoped it would help him, nevertheless.

He opened his eyes but still struggled to catch his breath. Panic gripped her. She ran to the kitchen and grabbed cold ginger and lemon tea from the fridge. She then ran back, sat him up, and brought the tea to his lips. The cool liquid calmed his breathing and seemed to stop the rasping. She sat with him, rubbing his back for a few minutes.

He put his hand on her knee and squeezed. "I think I'm okay, Chenoa. Thank you."

They sat quietly for a moment, watching the dogs eat. She continued to rub his back.

"Chayton, I'm really scared," she said after a while. "Where is everyone? What is happening?"

"I have no idea. I'm scared too." Tears welled up in his eyes.

Chenoa looked out the window and toward the dark skies and falling ash. It's Mordor, she thought. Chayton dozed off; his breathing steadied. She hesitantly reached for his hand and held it. She sat with him for the next few hours, staring out at the apocalypse outside their window.

When he woke, he rolled up from the bed, coughing and clearing mucus from his throat. He then turned and saw his sister. She sat on the edge of the bed, cradling her knees and rocking back and forth.

He put his hand on her back. "We'll be okay, Chenoa. I'm sure it's just the volcano messing everything up, and everyone is staying inside because of it." But he wasn't sure.

And she knew it.

Their pantry was still stocked with food. Their parents had filled it before leaving for Australia. Chenoa boiled some pasta and sauce over a flickering blue gas flame.

They had to use matches to light the gas. Machi shook the whole time, lying next to a pool of her own urine. She had been abused as a puppy and still suffered from that trauma. Chenoa put down a dog bed and gently moved Machi onto it. She cleaned up the yellow liquid with a dish towel.

"It's okay, girl," she said as she cradled Machi's face and gave her little kisses.

They ate at a table nook that had a large window, and the dogs huddled near their chairs.

This was always their favorite place to eat and play games. Decks of cards spread across the table, and Ticket to Ride and Monopoly sat at the end. No one liked to play Monopoly since Chenoa always won. The family wasn't sure if she was just lucky or if she somehow cheated without them being able to tell.

The window framed the view across their pool and the valley below. Ash continued to lightly rain down. The valley's usual thick green foliage was covered in gray tones like they were seeing it through a black-and-white photo. The late morning sun struggled to break through the cloudy skies.

The usual distant drone of motorbikes was absent. No trucks. No cars. Only sounds from their neighbor's chickens steadily reached their ears. A few insects chirped, but no birds made a single noise. It reminded them of when the animals fell silent during an eclipse a few years back.

They ate their food, chewing more slowly than usual, as they processed the situation. Even though they avoided eye contact with each other, they knew exactly how the other felt.

They tried their phones once more.

Nothing.

They stayed home for the next seven days, only opening the doors to let the dogs out to go to the bathroom. They had plenty of dry dog food to last them for months. The dogs usually also ate fresh chicken that was delivered frozen once a month, but no delivery came. No planes flew overhead, going south to the Ngurah Rai International Airport. Their days became a perpetual *Ethan Frome*—dark and silent—except with tropical temperatures.

They were alone and helpless.

They slept in the master bedroom with the dogs each night since it gave them more room and made them feel closer to their parents. Chayton and Chenoa slept on the bed, and the dogs slept nearby on the floor.

"Can't Kubi sleep in the bed with us?" she asked on the seventh night.

"Dad wouldn't like it."

"He isn't here, Chay."

"I know. But I still think they should sleep on the floor."

They fell asleep soon after. Chenoa awoke sometime later, checked to make sure her brother was still asleep, and then brought Kubi under the covers with her.

Chayton rose early the next day and wandered out into the living room. He never wore a watch, so he looked at his phone, which he still carried out of habit. It was just before seven a.m. As he looked out the window, he noticed that the sun was finally shining through the gray skies. No ash fell onto the ground.

He opened the front sliding doors and stepped out onto the ash-covered porch. Since no more ash fell, he decided to get rid of it. He grabbed a hose from around the corner to wash down the porch but reconsidered. They still had water from the water tank on the property, but he knew it would quickly run dry since the pump to the well was now off. He grabbed a broom instead and carefully moved the dust off the porch.

His dad would have done the same. He always cleaned when his world was out of control. There was comfort in a simple routine. *He would have been cleaning a lot these days*, Chayton thought.

Chayton walked out to the infinity pool that over-looked the valley, strolled around the edge, and gazed over the wall and into his neighbor's land to the south. No movement. He made his way to the back of his property, across the basketball court, and to the first gate. He could not see over the two-meter high, ironwood gate. Since soot and dirt had collected in the tracks, he needed two hands to slide it open. A truck and four scooters sat in the garage, covered in ash. He kept walking down the driveway and to the bottom gate. He then stood just inside the gate, straining to listen. No dogs barked, no chickens clucked, and no villagers buzzed by on their scooters.

He reached for the latch to open it but then pulled his hand back. He gazed through its opening instead and saw no movement. After checking the latch to make sure it's locked, he went back inside the house and closed the doors behind him.

Chayton and Chenoa sat on the porch, quietly eating Annie's mac and cheese. All the dogs lay around them. A light wind had picked up and blew north, up through the valley. The air was cooler than usual, and the ash had cleared. Spotted green doves and brown starlings had reappeared and played along the pool's edge.

"It's just like Nyepi," she said.

"I was thinking the same thing," he replied.

"Nyepi was Dad's favorite day." A bit of melancholy laced itself in her voice. "He loved it when the island stopped, and time just stood still. He always said he wished the whole world could have a Nyepi."

"Well, I think he got his wish," Chayton muttered.

The entire island would shut down on Nyepi, the Balinese New Year. No one was allowed to work, all electricity was shut off, and the internet and the TV would shut down. No one was allowed outside, but people would step out for air and stay away from the streets, where the village police patrolled. Since no motor vehicles were around, the air was cleaner. It was the only place in the world where the international airport would close. On that day, the world—for them—stopped.

Time stopped.

It was then that captivating sounds would emerge through the usual cacophony: the rushing river, the cawing birds, and the blowing wind through the valley. People had said it was the most restful and beautiful day they had ever experienced.

Chayton and Chenoa closed their eyes and listened.

Time had stopped.

But they strained to listen for human life.

Bright light shined in through the bedroom window for the first time in over two weeks. Chayton nudged Chenoa, and they went outside to find a clear blue sky. The air felt lighter and fresher. A pair of kingfishers—deep blue birds with a burnt orange chest and a long beak—sat in the frangipani tree near their pool. Its yellow and white flowers were in full bloom. A few birds flew around their thick, chubby branches. The area was electric with birds darting about the valley.

A young monkey sat high in a nearby coconut tree. He nibbled on some leaves and gazed down at the children below. Monkeys weren't common around their home. Their dad had seen one years ago with his friend, but they rarely ventured into the valley from their sanctuaries and the more remote forests up north.

Hundreds of herons filled the sky with their large wingspans, flying westward from their nesting home in Petulu.

"Chay, do you remember the story of the herons?" Chenoa asked, remembering the time they had visited there years earlier.

He had already been thinking about it as he watched the birds fly overhead. "Yeah. I remember." He began to retell the story they had learned in school.

In the 1960s, the Indonesian government systematically massacred members of the communist party, ethnic Chinese, and other supposed sympathizers. The genocide led to hundreds of thousands of deaths, possibly millions. Many bodies were never found, never given proper funeral rites. The dead's lost souls were left to wander this world.

It was a black stain on Indonesia's history to say the least.

Petulu, a tiny village just north of Ubud, held a ceremony to cleanse the village of the evil energy that lingered after the mass murder. One week later, the Kokokan—white herons—arrived in Petulu, and they had remained there ever since. The local story went that the wandering souls had used these birds as vessels and returned to Petulu. Locals believed that the herons brought the village a blessing of prosperity.

They watched as the birds disappeared over their home.

"Do you think they are carrying souls, Chayton?" Chenoa whispered. "That is a lot of birds."

He stared ahead, nodding and dropping his head. "Chenoa, I think we need to see what's up."

"You mean go out? Yeah, I'm thinking the same thing."

"Shall we drive, or do you want to walk?" he asked.

"Maybe we should drive in case something weird is out there."

"You read my mind."

CHAPTER 2

FEET

A LIGHT BREEZE carried the scent of blooming frangipanis. The trees' yellow and white flowers contrasted against the cobalt blue sky. A pair of doves cooed from the garden, and colorful butterflies and dragonflies danced through the bushes. Mother Nature was reawakening.

The kids crossed the basketball court at the rear of the house. The heavy ironwood gate groaned as they slid it open. The dogs barked and tried to push against the siblings' legs, probably believing they were finally going for a walk.

Chenoa, in the middle of the gateway, pushed them back with her leg. "Stay!"

They all sat, begrudgingly giving her puppy dog eyes.

Chayton threw a daypack with provisions into the truck's back seat and pulled himself into the cab. Their mom had purchased a 2011 Ford Ranger to transport the dogs for walks. The large truck came with search lights, oversized mag wheels, a step to get inside the cab, and a skull and crossbones on the hood. It did not exude a suburban mom style. She had turned heads as a blond mother driving a truck with a sordid past. Bikers would fist pump and honk as they passed.

The truck actually belonged to a head of Laskar, the largest gang on the island. The gang had started as a Hindu defense league after the first Bali bombing by Muslim extremists. Recently, they had just offered security and other services.

Their mom had painted the truck army green and adorned it with door and tailgate stickers that promoted Chayton's company, Junglo—a reforestation business he had set up with two of his former teachers from Green School. He had only been eighteen when he started it. His dad had joked that he hadn't started his own company until he was fifty.

Now, the truck advertised to no one except the stray dogs wandering the streets. The Instagram address directed viewers to nowhere.

Chayton backed out of the covered garage and turned the truck down the driveway and toward the lower gate that led out of the property. Green plants had grown over the driveway, crunching under the wheels. Orange and purple passion fruit hung from the garden trellis that their gardeners had built.

"Grab some fruit, Chenoa. Mom would be happy that you aren't eating chips," he quipped.

"Ha ha," she responded. She hopped out of the car and filled her shirt with the fallen fruit. She lumbered back to the car just as a few fruits rolled down the hill.

"Just leave them. We'll get them later. Now, open the gate," he directed.

"Why me? You're closer!"

"I'm driving, Chenoa. Just open it."

"Chayton, I really don't want to open the gate."

They always argued as to who should open the gate. But her hand was shaking, so he knew she wasn't being difficult.

"Okay," he conceded. "Hop in. I can do it." He reached behind him and grabbed the baseball bat that he had brought as protection.

Their dad kept bats near his bed. They had been robbed years prior, and the thieves had broken in through a door closest to the children's rooms. This had unsettled him, knowing that strange men had been just feet away from his children. So, he had gotten the bats as his own sense of safety.

Chayton examined the bat. It was an engraved Louisville Slugger with their dad's name on it from his time at EA Sports in Canada. EA had made a baseball video game called *Triple Play*, and the producer had given him the bat for his role as the head of marketing. Chayton ran his fingers along his dad's name. He squeezed his eyes tight, and a tear ran down his face.

"Chay, you okay?" Chenoa asked.

"Yeah. Just thinking about Dad."

He quickly opened and shut the truck door. Lifting the heavy latch, he peered through the opening. The gate groaned as it rolled along the metal trough.

A white flash darted by him. He yelled and swung the bat, clipping the gate and sending stinging vibrations through his hands.

"Chenoa!" he screamed.

A shadow edged out from behind the truck. She jumped into the back seat, straining to see what was there.

"Stay in the truck!" He crept to the back. As he turned the corner, he lifted the bat and jumped forward.

A white medium-sized dog coiled in fear.

He dropped the bat. "It's Piki, Chenoa."

Piki was their neighbor's dog that their mom had rescued from certain death. Chayton bent and rubbed his ears. He licked his face in return.

Chenoa got out of the truck and squealed as she hugged Piki. "Chayton, he's alive!"

"We're so happy to see you," he said as he buried his face in his collar, images of his mom coming to mind.

Piki was a sign of life. Not human but *life*. And he was family.

They put the dog in the back of the double-cab truck since he could provide some added protection. Their mood also lifted with their new companion. Chayton drove the truck out past the gate, and Chenoa slid the gate shut and ran back to the truck. She slammed and locked the car door. He slowly drove west, out onto the village road.

They passed their neighbor's compounds. No children played in the driveways. No women huddled together, preparing ceremonial offerings. They turned left onto Jalan Saraswati, the main road that led toward the cities of Ubud and Denpasar. A few chickens pecked the dirt. A small pack of dogs stepped out from a darkened doorway and watched them go by.

"Why aren't the dogs chasing the truck, Chayton?" Chenoa asked.

"I'm not sure," he said. "They look dopey and passive. But they aren't starving. I'd actually say they look healthier than usual."

"What's that?!" She pointed.

A mother pig and her piglets darted out from the rustling bushes. Pigs usually didn't run wild in Bali; they were confined to pens.

The children slightly lowered their windows to get some air and to listen for any signs of life. But the world was the quietest they had ever experienced. Birds chirped, and insects buzzed. An occasional rooster crowed. Chayton stopped the truck in the middle of the road and turned off the ignition.

Silence.

They both noticed the smell or lack thereof. The Balinese constantly burned things: leaves, garbage, and rice fields. It was cheaper than trying to legally dispose their garbage. Because of that, smoke often lingered in the air. At times, it was so dense that they needed to lock themselves in their home. But today was the first day they could ever remember where there wasn't pungent smoke. Nor did pleasant incense from the daily upacara offerings that were placed outside of every home, statue, and temple linger in the air. Instead, the air was pure and smelled earthy and clean. Piki stuck his head out the window, sniffing the most he could.

Chayton turned the ignition key and continued down the road. They scanned the side roads for any life.

He recalled years of watching action and horror movies with his dad that had left him wondering what lurked under his bed at night. He didn't even like spooky trailers. Even in his fifties, his dad would check under his bed. Chenoa was always the bravest when it came to horror movies.

But now he wondered when a zombie would come flying out of a nearby house and whether it would be a slow-moving George Romero zombie or an overly speedy

Zack Snyder one. He hoped for a Romero zombie since they could always outrun them. But those were a lot creepier and would sneak up and gnaw on their ankles.

He shook his head to clear his thoughts. *Zombies aren't real*, he thought. *Hopefully*. He rolled up his window just a touch, so a hand couldn't reach through, nevertheless.

Bali had already been quiet due to the covid lockdowns. They had wreaked havoc on the world, sending hundreds of millions of people into poverty. Their dad had been unable to get back to Bali from California for over ten months since airports and consulates shut. He had missed Chayton's high school graduation and everyone's birthdays, but he made it back just before Christmas. No foreign tourists came to Bali for over two years. Their ten million visitors a year had dropped to zero. The economy had been devastated. Bali had already felt postapocalyptic with no visitors and eighty percent of their businesses shutting down.

But at least there had been some people and activity on the streets. Now, there was nothing. Not one single person.

Chenoa touched her hand to Chayton's shoulder. He slowed the truck as she pointed to a doorway off to the right. A sandaled foot lay at an angle just inside the door frame. He pulled alongside the home's entrance. She rolled down her window, and he turned off the truck.

"Hello?!" she yelled out. "Hello there! We are from Villa Jati. Are you okay? Can we come in?"

"Thank god there are people, Chenoa," he muttered.

The person moved their foot, getting ready to stand.

"Hi, there!" she yelled, smiling. "We are so happy to see you. Are you all okay?!"

The foot spasmed. Both feet thrust, pulling the body inside the entrance. But the movement was too unnatural. Something had moved them.

She screamed, and Chayton pushed back against his seat. Piki barked and tried to jump through the half-open window. The feet flopped again but then stopped moving. A grand shadow emerged in the doorframe.

"Chenoa, roll up your window!" he commanded.

She fumbled to turn the handle. A large black dog bolted out of the doorway and toward their truck. He leaped into the back seat to roll up Piki's window. The black dog hit Chenoa's window, and blood and saliva smeared on the glass.

They now understood why they hadn't seen any bodies around. And why the animals looked so well fed.

They swerved away, and the dog chased the truck. After a few moments, Chayton watched the dog in his rearview mirror as it turned and went back inside the home.

"What the hell was that?!" his sister yelled. "Was the dog eating that person?"

"I don't know," he snipped. "That dog had blood all over its face!" His hands shook. He wanted to console her, but he also wanted to be consoled.

He wanted his parents back.

"I'm sorry, Chenoa," he said after a deep breath. "I think the animals are just eating what they can find. It explains why we aren't seeing any other people. Remember how we learned how quickly the tropics consumed things? But I don't know why everyone seems to have died in the first place. Why are we still alive, but everyone else is dead?"

She sat quietly, shaking and holding back tears.

They continued down the road. Monkeys crowded a local fruit and vegetable stand. Even though monkeys weren't common around here, they had already been making their way into major towns since all the businesses had closed over the past two years. But now they had free rein.

The truck continued down the road, through a T-junction, and pulled in front of a convenience store. They often stopped here to pick up chocolate, ice cream, or snacks for movie nights at home. They looked at each other, silently questioning whether they should go in. He pulled into the parking area, and they looked around before getting out of the truck. They decided to leave Piki behind but grabbed the baseball bats.

The front door had been left ajar. Moldy and musty air hit them as they stepped inside. They found some comfort in being in a store with shelves of unhealthy snacks. A tear ran down Chenoa's cheek as she thought about how they would never again sit together as a family, eating snacks or ice cream from here while watching *Ted Lasso* or *Modern Family*.

Chayton moved toward the shop's back door and turned the handle. Stacks of dry food and large Balian water containers sat next to gas containers that were used to run stoves and water heaters. He grabbed a few water and gas containers and set them near the front door.

"We should keep our supplies at home," he said. "Let's fill some bags with snacks, and we'll get out of here."

They found cloth bags and filled them with chips, chocolate, instant noodles, and drinks. They grabbed what they could and ran to the truck, placing everything in the back. After returning to get the water and gas containers, they loaded them into the truck's bed.

They then sat in the truck, eating chips and cookies. Piki panted behind them with his nose out a crack in the window. They eagerly munched on the snacks, eating beyond their hunger. Snacks like this were usually treats, but now they felt like necessities for their souls. Chenoa offered Piki a few chips, which he eagerly gobbled up.

Afterward, fear came rushing back to Chayton. "What is going on?" he asked, white knuckles gripping the steering wheel.

"I don't know! I don't know," she replied. An orange ring had formed around her mouth from the Doritos.

Chayton opened his mouth but then stopped.

They both knew their dad would have commented on their swearing. He had said it was okay to swear as long as they could master the art. His London friend was a gifted swearer with his proper English accent. He could make the F- and C-words sound almost poetic. Their mom had found it funny when English people swore since it didn't sound as bad as when a Canadian or an American blurted out an expletive. But everyone wasn't meant to swear. This, however, seemed like the perfect time to drop a few F-bombs.

They drove to the end of the road. To the left was the cultural center of Bali named Ubud, a funky little town with people wearing lululemon tights and discussing the alignment of their chakras. Their dad had described it as the Berkeley of Asia. To the right was the direction to Denpasar, the main city of Bali. It was also the road to Green School where they had both attended.

After debating for a while, they decided they'd had enough for one day. Chayton turned the truck around and headed back home. They drove in silence the rest of the way. Only when they approached the turn back into their driveway did Chenoa yell.

"Chayton!"

"What, Chenoa?!" He slammed on the breaks. "Stop yelling!"

"What about the bears?!"

CHAPTER 3

FREE

"WHAT ABOUT THE bears, Chayton?!" Chenoa yelled.

"Jesus, Chenoa. Quit yelling. What bears?"

"Don't say Jesus. Grandpa wouldn't like it."

"Well, he isn't here at the moment. What *bears*?"

"The bears at the elephant park," she said as if it was simple. "You know where we went with Mom and Dad? What if they are still in their cages? What if the elephants are still chained up?"

He put the truck in park. It was already early afternoon, and it hadn't been the most relaxing day with the blood-faced dog and the flopping feet. He wanted to go home. But he knew she was right, and he didn't want the animals to suffer.

"Okay. Let's go," he said. "But they may already be dead." He regretted the words the moment they crossed his lips.

Chenoa stared straight ahead, her lips quivering.

"I'm sorry. I shouldn't have said that." He hesitated. "You're...you're just like Mom. If she was here, she'd be going from house to house, feeding all the animals. She'd be proud of you." He put the car in drive. "Let's go."

"Thanks, Chayton," Chenoa replied with a stuttered sigh.

As his sister said his name, his time in Japan came to mind, and he chuckled. "Chenoa, do you remember how Mom and Dad named us?"

She paused for a moment, struggling to recall it. "It's a bit blurry."

"I was a girl for the first ten minutes of my life," he began. "Mayumi-san was the midwife, but her English wasn't very good. 'You have a beautiful baby girl,' she had said when I was delivered. But when Dad picked me up, he saw I had a wiener—"

"A penis," Chenoa interrupted.

"Oh, brother. Okay. A penis," he repeated. "Mom said that naming kids was such a pain in the ass. One of their friends said that they shouldn't call me Chayton because it sounded like Satan in Saudi Arabia. People get worked up about too much shit in the world."

"Not anymore," she commented.

He let out his boisterous laugh that everyone loved. "No kidding. It all seems so unimportant right now. But at least they didn't call me Bertha or Karl. Everyone seems to know a problematic Bertha or Karl."

She chuckled.

"Mom and Dad were watching the Spiderman movie with me in her belly. She didn't like action movies much then. Dad must have tricked her to go."

"You mean like when he tricked her to go to Disneyland?" added.

"Yep. Probably the same tactic. But as the credits rolled, she had asked, 'What about Maguire as a name?' She was talking about Toby Maguire. Dad felt it would make a better middle name. They had found my name, Chayton, on the internet. Dad liked Native American culture for some reason and found the Sioux name that meant *falcon*. Their couple friends, Ross and Mike, stopped any discussion on the order of the names since they had already named their Christmas tree Chayton Maguire Thompson."

"That is a lot of work for a name, Chay. I'm just going to name my kid John or Mary when I..." She trailed off.

They both realized the futility of her comment.

"What about my name, Chay? Tell me the story." She already knew the story but found hearing her brother reminisce comforting.

"You were born at home in Singapore with just mom, dad, and a doula standing by. Dad caught you. I came in just after. There is a picture somewhere of me sleeping beside you on your first day. Your middle name is Jati from Uncle John, Dad's brother. He had died young from brain cancer. His friends would call him JT, pronounced *jay-tee*, for John Thompson. Dad wrote it out as Jati, which means teakwood in Balinese and is a Sanskrit term for the cycle of life and death. Chenoa is also an American Indian name that means white dove."

Chenoa thought about how different their lives were from people who grew up in the US or Canada. She had spent her entire life in Asia. Animal- and pet-loving Westerners didn't always like how animals were treated here. Some Asians ate dogs, which appalled them. But Asians rightly saw the hypocrisy as Westerners ate everything else. *Why should dogs be any different to a cow or a pig?* she thought. But still... "I'm glad the dogs are still alive, Chay."

"What are you on about?"

"Dogs. I'm glad there are still dogs around and that they don't have to worry about being kicked or eaten by people. Mom was the best with them. I think she did more to help them than anyone else. I mean, who knew Bali dogs were one of the oldest dog species in the world?"

"Dr. Goodall knew. Remember when Dad helped bring her over to Bali when he ran Green School? She hated how animals were abused at the Bali Zoo and on the dolphin tours up north."

"I hope she is with her chimps in Africa," Chenoa said. "That makes me happy to think of her with the animals she loved."

Chayton pulled over next to a warung, a small family-owned business, along the roadside. A monkey perched itself along the roof's edge and peeled a banana. The siblings got out and rifled through the boxes to find food for the bears. Rotten and half-eaten fruit lay along the ground.

"Here are some watermelons," Chenoa called.

They loaded them all into the truck. She grabbed papaya from a tree next to the truck.

Dogs, chickens, ducks, and pigs wandered along the roads. Chayton observed a pig standing firm in the street. He honked, but the animal just stared at the front of the car. He sensed an understanding in the pig's eyes, a knowing. *Did they realize their masters were gone?* he thought.

"It's kind of like *Animal Farm*," she said. "That pig has a different attitude. Not sure you remember, Chay, but it didn't turn out so well at the end of that novel. If I see pigs sitting and playing cards at tables in empty homes, I'm swimming off this island."

"That wouldn't be the strangest thing that's happened in the past few weeks," he murmured.

He drove by the park's entrance, noticing the foliage that had grown across the road. The rice fields rippled in the afternoon breeze as the sun moved toward the horizon. He backed up and turned into a dirt driveway. The truck lurched as he wandered off the covered roadway, so he pulled the wheel back to the center.

A male elephant blocked their path.

Chenoa smiled, got out of the car, picked some grass from the side of the road, and approached the front of the elephant. She held out the grass. The elephant wrapped his trunk around it and put it into his mouth.

"There, there," she muttered as she rubbed its trunk.

She had ridden elephants in Bali, Thailand, and Sri Lanka. She was comfortable around them. She moved to the side and massaged his ear. The animal gently swung his head from side to side, soothed by the contact. He then lifted his foot, creating a metallic rattle. She turned her head toward the noise. Held by a simple bolt and fastener, a short, heavy chain was wrapped around his rear foot.

The animal rubbed her face with his trunk. She giggled as he tickled her neck.

She turned back toward her brother. "He's friendly, Chay. But he has a chain around his leg."

"They always kept them chained up at night. I bet he broke away from the pens down below."

He made his way to the elephant's back foot and reached down to release the chain. Years of confinement had abraded the animal, leaving a lengthy scar that was oddly shaped like the Nike swoosh on his inner leg. The elephant turned his head in the boy's direction and reached his trunk out to him. He rubbed the trunk as Chenoa brought more grass to feed the elephant.

"You are beautiful," she said as she looked into his eyes. "We'll take care of you and check on your family. Just be still."

The chain fell to the ground, and Chayton stepped away. The elephant lifted his leg and swung his trunk back and forth.

"I think he's dancing, Chenoa!" He laughed. "Run along, Swoosh."

The elephant moved into the grass, turning back once to look upon the children. He raised his trunk and trumpeted.

"Look, Chenoa." He pointed toward the elephant pen down below. "The rest are all still chained up. And there is a baby."

The elephants stood in a row under a simple bamboo structure and a corrugated iron roof. They shifted their weight back and forth, restless and aggravated from their confinement.

He knew elephants could live for days without food, but they still needed a water source. A water trough ran in front of the elephants, continuously filled from a running tap.

"Maybe one of the keepers had turned it on," his sister suggested. "But why hadn't they just released the elephants? Were they going to come back?"

They gathered piles of grass and tossed them to the elephants. The elephants greedily shoved them into their mouths. They repeated the feeding a few times, awaiting the animals to calm down.

Chenoa then stood in front of the elephants, speaking in gentle tones. Chayton made his way along the line and released the chains from each. They lumbered into the grassy fields and continued to feed. The baby wove in and out of her mom's legs, and Swoosh rejoined the group.

Chenoa remembered how their dad had often spoken about his time on the safari in Africa. Unlike animals in a zoo, those wild animals were bolder and more confident. He had even joked that the rabbits had an attitude.

The elephants moved more into the fields to forage for food. The children smiled, witnessing the creatures roam free for the first time in their lives.

Then the reason why they had come hit Chenoa. "Chayton! The bears!"

"Oh yeah," he muttered. "The bears."

They ran to the truck and drove to the chocolate shop near the bear pens. Piki stayed in the truck as they grabbed the watermelons and papaya and sprinted to the cement railing that encircled the two enclosed areas. The large pens had many trees and a small hill to climb in the middle. A hole replicating a cave had been dug into the side of the hill for the sun bears to sleep. An iron door separated the male's pen from the mother and baby's pen.

The male sun bear clamored to the wall as he saw the kids. Mud and what appeared to be blood matted the hair on his head. Rotting fruit littered the pen where it appeared the keepers had thrown food in before fleeing. They tossed two melons to the bear, and he ripped them open and devoured the juicy fruit.

The mother hovered over the baby, who lay panting on his side. They threw three melons into their pen, and the mother bit into the first and devoured the fruit. She bit into the second, ate half, and then carried the melon over to her baby. She rocked him, and his eyes fluttered. His tongue snaked out, licking the fruit that lay by his head. He nibbled and then rolled onto his belly, shoving his face into the fruit.

The siblings emptied the rest of the fruit from the car into the pens and opened the taps that led to the water troughs below.

"I panicked that they would be dead," Chenoa admitted. "But what do we do now?"

"Let's let them out," her brother said. "They can't stay here in the pens, and we can't come up here every day. They have tons of food to eat with all the fruit on the island. Why not let them out? What's going to happen? We get in trouble?"

They made their way to the gate on the other side of the pen. The mother's nose appeared through the gap next to the latch. The baby clawed at the door and nuzzled his head next to his mom.

"Oh, they're so cute!" Chenoa gushed.

"Yeah, and they got teeth and claws," Chayton responded.

"How are we going to do this?" she asked.

They found a hose and drove the truck to the road near the gate.

"We can tie the hose to the gate, unlock the latch, and pull the door open," he suggested. "I'll be in the truck ready to drive."

They secured the hose and unlocked the latch. She counted down with her fingers as she readied to pull the gate open. But the door flew open early, startling her, and the mother bear charged.

"Run, Chenoa!" her brother screamed. "Run!"

She sprinted toward the truck. She glanced back once to see the bear closing in, and her foot caught on a root. She rolled and covered her head, awaiting the attack. The ground shook as the bear continued to charge. She tucked in her knees and cradled her head.

Piki bolted from the open door of the truck. He charged over Chenoa and stood between the bear and the cowering girl. Saliva flew from the dog's mouth as he bared his fangs. The bear pulled back within a few feet and skidded to a halt. She reared and roared. Piki moved to keep himself between Chenoa and the bear. But the baby came to his mother's side, and the mother fell onto all fours. She lowered her head, and they moved into the forest.

Chayton ran over to Chenoa and helped her up. Images from *The Revenant*, where a grizzly had ripped a man to pieces, flooded his mind. "Chenoa, Chenoa. Are you hurt?" He picked her up and cradled her.

He couldn't handle the idea of losing his sister. He didn't always show it, but he loved her. Mud covered her face, and he felt her heart pounding through his chest.

"I'm okay, Chayton," she panted. "And thank you, Piki. Thank you." She buried her face in his fur.

They still had the male bear to let out but didn't want to deal with another charging attack. Chayton unlatched the gate and ran to the car. The bear nudged the door open and walked out of the pen on his own. He then glanced at the children and dog in the truck. He approached them but turned and moved into the forest.

The siblings sat in silence for some time, staring into the forest. Long shadows from the trees stretched in front of them.

"Let's head home, Chenoa," Chay said.

"Look, Chayton!" She pointed.

The herd of elephants had moved across the rice fields, heading south. Which was also the direction of the children's home. The female led the group, and the baby walked in the center of the herd, protected. As the children drove past the elephants, Swoosh raised his head and flipped his trunk.

Chayton wished his parents were there.

Chenoa had the same thought.

CHAPTER 4

LIONS AND TIGERS AND BEARS

SINCE CHAYTON AND Chenoa's half-hectare home had an organic garden and edible plants growing for miles, food wasn't on the top of their list. Mango, papaya, and durian hung from their trees; herbs and medicinal plants grew in the gardens.

But they dug more garden beds for tomatoes, cassava, kale, eggplant, and cucumbers. Bali was always warm and humid, so most plants could grow year-round as the four seasons were wet, wetter, hot, and hotter.

They also built a makeshift pen enclosure on their neighbor's land next door. That land was flat, and their common wall cut the amount of needed building. They cut moringa branches and planted them in rows to create a living fence, which would grow and intertwine over time. This wasn't necessary for the cows as they didn't wander as long as there was food. Pigs would explore and move away. The fence offered them some comfort though, and it gave them a project to do.

They cut bamboo for a chicken coop and ensured that they didn't build it under the falling coconuts, which would destroy the coop and possibly kill the chickens. It wasn't uncommon to hear of people or animals dying from falling coconuts in Bali.

Since nature had rebalanced from the lack of human consumption, an overabundance of fruit grew. The fallen fruit provided feed for the pigs, along with the birds and other creatures of the night.

"Chenoa, what are those?" Chayton pointed at some black-and-white-banded, catlike creatures in the coffee forest ahead of them.

"Civets. You know, Luwaks. They eat the coffee beans and fruit and then poop out the hard seeds. Locals would collect them and sell them for a ridiculous price to ignorant tourists. I remember Asher, who started FREAK coffee, telling me that it was all a big hoax."

In *The Bucket List*, Jack Nicholson had explained to Morgan Freeman that he hadn't lived until he had Luwak coffee, which made it famous. And locals had no shame when tourists would pay five times the price for turd-affected coffee beans. People could be fools.

They took a break from the midday heat and made fresh lemonade mixed with mint and sugarcane.

"I wish we had ice," Chenoa said, licking her lips. "Oh, I would die to have some ice right now."

"Now I want ice. I wish you didn't mention it."

She drank her lemonade, longing for the cool tingle of an icy drink on her throat.

Chayton looked over. The pool had turned green with algae since the pump had stopped. He considered keeping the generator running, but it was too much effort, and he wanted to keep it available for an unforeseen emergency.

They agreed to convert the pool into a pond. Chenoa brought water lilies and koi from the village temple. Their neighbor had a tilapia fishpond. The water level had dropped there, but the fish were alive. She knew they weren't native fish but were common enough. The fish would give them a food supply and keep the mosquito larvae at bay.

"It's sad," Chayton said once they were almost finished. "Dad wouldn't like this. He was in this pool every day. The first thing he did every morning was dive into the pool to wake up."

"Naked," she offered.

"Yeah. He did that. Luckily, the neighbors couldn't see in. He sure loved this pool though."

"I'd wake up early sometimes and would hear the slap of his arms against the water as he trained." She paused, her smile falling. "I miss them, Chay. I really miss them."

He nodded. Each day was a struggle as their little successes competed with their memories of loss.

They sipped their drinks, watching the pool.

As the days passed, birds came by each day and bathed in the pool's edge. Frogs sat on the lily pads. Herons would stalk the edge, dipping their heads in for frogs. Brilliant blue kingfishers bathed, diving into the water, fluttering, and then returning to the fragrant frangipani tree. Dragonflies also returned to the area, surveying the water for smaller insects.

Chayton swam in the pool to cool from the midday sun. He didn't mind the other *animals* swimming around. Chenoa joined him but remained horizontal and kept her feet tucked up from the bottom, not wanting to step on anything slithering in the depths.

Since their water tank had run dry, they could no longer pump water from the deep well. Instead, the rain had maintained the water levels, and the lilies reduced evaporation.

They decided to run a water line into the pool to provide circulation and oxygen to the fish. They had located the government water lines and extended the pipe to their water main by using PVC piping from the tool shed. The natural ponds sat well above the property, so gravity played its role to allow them to top off the pool, shower, and get water to the sinks and toilets. With no human or pesticide pollution, they had little concern for the quality of the water.

The natural springs brimmed and overflowed, reforming some rivulets from centuries past. The water itself seemed to have memory, and little by little, it expanded its usual course and reforged new paths down to the river.

"Chayton?" Chenoa asked out of the blue.

"Don't say it, Chenoa. I know what you're thinking. We can't let the animals out of the zoo."

"How do you know that's what I am thinking?" she challenged.

"Because I saw that drawing you made of the lions over there." He pointed to a picture of lions in cages that sat on their outside table.

"We can't let them die!"

He knew he wouldn't win this discussion. He also wanted to free the animals, but his sister had almost died by letting out a bear. What would happen if the lions, tigers, and other creatures that eat humans were released? *They are probably already dead anyway*, he thought.

Their truck moved along the empty streets. A few dogs and farm animals loitered along the roadside. He spotted a dead body but didn't mention it. He saw his sister put her head down, however, turning away from the body. *Sometimes, things don't need to be discussed*, he thought. *What does it help to talk about another half-eaten dead body?*

The rotten smell of decomposing bodies hung in the air. Nature was taking its course as animals and microbes fed on the corpses. Vines crawled across the bodies, pushing them back into the earth. They also snaked up the buildings, weaving into the gaps and pulling at the structures. A tree branch pushed into the side of one wall, and a crack had formed toward the base. The wall would fall soon, but the tree would continue its upward journey toward the sun.

Nature was unabashedly reclaiming itself, eliminating humans' achievements.

Chayton avoided the debris on the road. The trip was only thirty minutes, half of what it usually took. A macaque sat on the park entrance sign like a lookout. Its head followed the truck as it turned into the drive. Once inside the park, Chayton's and Chenoa's mouths dropped at the sight of elephants, giraffes, rhinos, and many other animals wandering outside the gates.

"Where is David Attenborough when you need him?" she commented.

They drove directly into the park since the metal gates were wide open. She noticed a flyer flopping against a gate. She opened her mouth to mention it to her brother but stopped herself as a gazelle leaped across their hood, followed by a pursuing black leopard.

Every cage was *open*. The scene before them was more of an open savanna than a zoo as all varieties of animals roamed around. Chayton maneuvered along the wide pedestrian paths, avoiding peacocks, otters, antelope, and an alligator who had taken refuge near a drinking fountain. Like in the villages, trees and shrubs took over the cages and paths. Nature had grown tired of humanity's ignorance and abuse and made it clear that humankind wasn't at the top of the food chain.

Humankind was dead, and the animals now ruled.

Chayton finished the loop, heading back to the main entrance. As they passed the empty chimpanzee exhibit, he said, "Chenoa, there are your lions. Happy now? All the animals are out of their cages. They must have let them go."

A herd of elephants wandered out of the main gates. But the lions blocked their path, forcing him to slow to a stop. He honked the horn in an attempt to spook them, but the jarring sound just sent the monkeys into a wild cacophony.

"Chayton!" Chenoa chastised. "Don't do that. You're frightening them."

"How are we supposed to get them to move?" He pressed the horn again. Yet he wasn't impatient—just scared. He didn't know how they'd get home through the unsettling roaming animals. He slowly drove forward, hoping the lions would disperse.

Chenoa screamed as the truck jolted. A golden mane filled the frame of his rearview mirror. Two piercing amber eyes stared into his but were soon replaced by gaping jaws and teeth as a roar shook the cab.

He turned his head to see a full lion head behind the fogged glass. "Don't move, Chenoa. Just don't move."

Claws scraped the window and the metallic framing. The lion jumped onto the roof and then down onto the hood, where he perched himself. His tail whipped across the front windshield. He seemed to have lost interest in the children, now focused on a small herd of deer.

The pride mechanically shifted their gaze from the truck to the deer. A female had broken away from the pride and crawled in the deer's direction. Chenoa noticed two others had circled around to the back of the herd. The muscles on the back of the male on their hood rippled as the entire pride bolted. The truck lurched as he jumped.

The first female tackled a stray from the back of the herd. A female pair corralled the leader, ripping into its throat and hindleg. The male charged at the solo female standing over her fallen prey. She roared but conceded to the larger male. Blood flew from the deer's neck as its still-beating heart gave its last few pumps. The golden faces turned crimson, flesh and fur hung from their jaws.

As Chayton drove past the feeding pride, the male turned his head to stare at the boy. "I got the message, sir. I know who is the king," he murmured. He pressed the accelerator a bit harder to scoot past the lions.

"Stop, Chay," Chenoa said. "There is something written on that paper on the gate." She opened the door to get out.

He grabbed her. "What are you doing? Mufasa and Scar are over there. Just hold on."

He maneuvered the truck to drive next to the flapping paper, and she quickly rolled the window down to snatch it before spinning the handle closed. She read the letter to her brother.

I tried to feed the animals but ran out of food. I did my best, but I just couldn't do it anymore. I am alone and can't breathe well. My family is gone. Everyone is gone. I hid from the lions behind the metal door. I am going to let the tigers out next. Please tell my family I love them.

Is anyone reading this? What has happened? Am I the last person left?

—Nyoman

Tears and dirty fingerprints stained the paper. The edges were crumpled from desperate hands holding onto the last hope of humanity.

Chenoa felt it was odd—even sad—that the letter was written in English. Even in the end, the impact of tourism was still prevalent.

The children did not discuss the letter. Instead, she put it back onto the gate. She smoothed it out flat and straightened the bent edges as best as she could. She then whispered a few words, a last tribute to Nyoman and his family. And to everyone else.

They drove away from the park. Lions lazed in the rice fields. Orangutans lounged near a Bodhi tree. Something moved through the long rice grass, reminding Chayton of the velociraptors stalking the humans in *Jurassic Park*. *What is hunting us?* he thought.

The animals were free and had plenty of food, more than they could consume. They would populate the island quickly enough.

The same monkey as before watched them drive away from the exit. Chenoa thought she saw it wave at them in good riddance. *Darwin would've loved this*, she thought. *And humans clearly weren't the fittest.*

Bali was wild again.

CHAPTER 5

THE MONKEY KING

"WHERE ARE YOU going, Chay?" Chenoa asked one morning.

"Why don't we drive into Ubud and see if anything is there?" Chayton suggested.

"Haven't you had your fill of wild Bali? There used to be a few snakes and rabid dogs. Now we have lions and tigers and bears chasing us."

"Oh my!" he sang cheekily, mimicking Dorothy from *The Wizard of Oz*.

They both laughed. They hadn't laughed much over the past couple of weeks. Being the last two people left on Earth didn't leave much to laugh about.

"All right, Chay," she said, giving in. "Let's go check it out."

Ubud was Bali's spiritual center. Yogis would sit cross-legged in restaurants, wannabee yogis would listen attentively, and newly trained yogis would impose their knowledge onto others. Digital nomads would huddle in cafés, sipping their cold coffee in false belief that the staff didn't know they were only there for the internet. Ever since *Eat, Pray, Love* hit the bookshelves, people had flocked to Bali either to find love...or to get divorced.

Their truck rumbled into Ubud. Lockdowns had silenced Bali as businesses shuttered, and people stayed home, unemployed. Ubud had become a literal ghost town. As they drove along empty, lightless streets, they didn't feel much difference from when the island had suffered. The exception was that they knew the streets would never be busy again.

When they had first come to Bali from Singapore, Chenoa was three, and Chayton was seven. Ubud was their hometown. People called it a city, but it was more like a large village with a population of seventy thousand.

They passed Mama Mia and Taco Casa. The two usually bustling restaurants were now empty and still, except for the monkeys that sat on the tables and the bats that hung from the ceiling. They had eaten at Taco Casa so often that Chenoa had her own burrito—a Chenoa Burrito—which the staff knew was black beans, guacamole, cheese, and red rice.

Chayton turned onto Monkey Forest Road, named after the famous monkey sanctuary enroute. He chuckled to himself as he realized that he was still concerned about the direction of traffic and driving on the left side of the road.

No one had actually followed the driving rules in Bali. They drove the wrong way, passed on the inside, exited blindly from the side roads, and parked anywhere and in any direction. They even drove scooters without helmets and rarely used their blinkers. People bought their driver's license to bypass the test. One Indonesian friend of their dad's had requested to take the written and driving test. The staff had struggled to find the official form, and the driving test consisted of driving forward ten meters and back ten meters. Bali was a lawless society when it came to driving.

Chenoa pointed out the half-hanging sign for Hubud, the first coworking space in Bali and Dad's old work. Bali was a mecca for digital nomads. They flocked there for the weather, the beaches, and the affordable lifestyle.

"Remember the Halloween parties and FuckUp Nights at Hubud?" Chenoa asked. FuckUp Nights allowed people to share their failures and vulnerabilities in front of a live audience.

"I remember Mona dropping about fifty F-bombs and then apologizing to Dad for her swearing frenzy. Everyone had laughed. I think we were lucky to be around so many fun and interesting people. I would give anything to be at an event with people tonight."

They passed the monkey forest sanctuary, which dated back to the fourteenth century. Tall, green trees overtook the area and shaded the road. Up ahead was a small statue of monkeys cleaning each other's backs. Chenoa recalled a tour she had taken at the forest. The sanctuary was created in accordance with the Hindu principle of Tri Hita Karana: harmony between humans, god, and the natural world. *Now it is only needed to bring harmony between god and the natural world with no more people*, she thought.

"Remember that guy when the monkey jumped on him and got shit all over his clean white shirt?" Chayton asked. "What was he thinking? Same as all the new families who start at Green School and try to keep their clothes sparkly white the first year. Nothing stays white in Bali."

"Chay, where are all the monkeys?"

"Who knows? Maybe the lions ate them," he offered sarcastically.

The nearby shops were empty. Medicinal tinospora vines crawled up the paint-peeled walls. The windows stared, blank and dead. A pristine green and white Starbucks sign hung conspicuously above the shop. Unlike all the other signs extending up the road, this one held its shape and tone. Even long after people were gone, Starbucks was still promoting its brand.

Chayton found irony in the fact that while Starbucks had the most shops in the world, their market share was the same as the mom-and-pop shop on the corner. He slowed the truck next to the coffee shop. His parents used to love Starbucks. His dad would argue that it was fashionable for people to not like them. He wasn't a fan of the corporate world, but he also didn't have a problem with the coffee chain. He loved the service, the ambiance, and the coffee—especially the pumpkin spice lattes for Thanksgiving. Chayton liked Starbucks and wasn't bothered when someone gave him a lecture on the demerits of the company.

"If someone makes fun of your tastes in songs, clothing, books, or movies, just smile and ignore them," Dad would say. "Life is too short to put up with people telling you what to do and how to think. Just be yourself."

And his dad was true to his word. He was a huge fan of the rock band, Kiss, and the punk band, Dead Kennedys. He even enjoyed *Pitch Perfect* 2.

Chayton pulled the car over and got out. He grabbed the baseball bats from the back seat, and he locked the door.

"What did you do that for?" Chenoa asked. "Who is going to steal anything from us?"

"Just shut up. You're an idiot."

"Ass crack."

They walked side by side, their heads scanning back and forth. She looked backward occasionally as she imagined something sneaking up on them. They had played baseball on the field across the road and watched the burning of ogoh-ogoh to dispatch evil spirits during the Nyepi ceremony. The field had never had the chance to recover from humans' endless trampling. But now the lush, overgrown grass stood knee high.

Chayton put his hand out to stop Chenoa as they stood at the field's edge. He scanned the field and the neighboring building. Tutmak, Ubud's oldest restaurant, quietly sat on the northeast corner. He winced as he saw the now dead library, where they would check out books with their parents, straight across the field.

"Why are we stopping?" she asked.

"Maybe something is in the grass like at the zoo."

"Don't be a moron," she responded and ran into the grass.

He reached for her but missed. "Chenoa!" he yelled as he ran in after her.

The grass rippled behind him and then arced around his side and toward his sister.

"Chenoa! Stop! Please," he pleaded.

A shadow flashed above the library fifty meters away. More shadows darted across the frozen yogurt shop to his left, halfway to the library. The ripple in the grass closed in on Chenoa.

"Jesus, Chenoa. Stop! Something is chasing you!"

A humanlike silhouette rose atop the library. He raised his hand to wave but then saw that the image was *not* human. It flew from atop the building and landed in the field, disappearing in the long grass. Chenoa froze as she saw the creature leap. Her brother reached her, panting. Whatever had been following her moved toward the oncoming creature in the grass.

"Get down!" he commanded, pulling her to the ground.

She shook next to him. They saw nothing except for the grass swaying in front of them.

"Just be quiet," he whispered. "They can't see us."

The grass parted inches from their faces. Slit, pale green eyes emerged. Gaping jaws widened, showing off razor teeth and large canines. Chenoa diverted her eyes, knowing not to directly stare into the eyes of a macaque since they saw it as a challenge. She flicked at her brother's knee for him to follow. The children froze, heads between their knees.

"Let's run, Chenoa," he whispered.

"No."

She knew he was impulsive. Teachers loved him, but he was often a distraction in class. In middle school, one of his teachers told him to run around the field if he was feeling energetic. He created a YouTube channel with his friends entitled Chayton Tries that had hits such as "Chayton Tries Some Purple Shit" and "Chayton Tries Sparkling Water Gone Wrong." He was a jokester and made people laugh. He'd entertain his parents with his goofy dance moves. So, Chenoa knew what would happen next.

"Chay, no."

He looked up into the eyes of the male monkey. The monkey howled, and his jaws widened to the height of the boy's head. Saliva flew into his face, and a putrid stench filled his nostrils. He gagged. The monkey's breath smelled of death, and he wondered if the monkey was eating humans. The male hissed and punched the ground.

Chayton started to lift his bat, but she moved her hand to stop him. The monkey grabbed the boy's long, blond, curly hair and yanked it, throwing his head to the side. He then pushed the boy backward. He turned to the girl, gently pulling on her hair. Another smaller monkey jumped onto Chayton's chest as he lay on his back, and a warm, pungent liquid ran down his arm.

The little bastard just pissed on me, he thought.

They remained still for what felt like an hour as the monkeys prodded and pushed them, only to lose interest and slowly disperse. But the king remained seated near them. Chayton sat up next to Chenoa. They both cradled their legs and kept their eyes downward. The king grunted and gently touched the back of their hands. Huffing, he disappeared into the grass.

They stay quiet for another twenty minutes. She then gestured to him, and they made their way back to the truck and slammed the doors shut.

"Holy shit. Holy shit!" he yelled. "That asswipe pissed on me!"

"That's what you're worried about? They were getting ready to eat us, and you are worried about a little monkey pee? You've had geckos crapping on you for years, and there is dog poop everywhere. The school had compost toilets that had poo and pee all over them since boys can't aim. I think you are missing the point here."

"Yeah. What's that?" he snipped.

"We are *alive*, you doofus. Let's get the hell out of here and go home. I've had it with wildlife for one day.

Jeez. Can it get any weirder? I think I peed my pants," she blurted.

"I don't know how it can get any weirder. I really don't know how," he muttered as he pulled away and headed toward their home.

As they turned left off Monkey Forest Road and onto Jalan Raya, Chenoa glimpsed a huge gray presence in the middle of the street. A mother rhino and her baby trotted down the road, passing by Dairy Queen and Bank Mandiri.

"And there it is," she said, shaking her head.

CHAPTER 6

NORMALCY

"WHAT ARE YOU doing, Chenoa?" Chayton asked as she sat on the floor of the media room.

She held a hefty leather-bound, gold-lettered book that sagged in her lap. "Reading. Gandalf is fighting the Balrog. It was Dad's favorite scene."

Their dad was a bit of a nerd. He loved books and movies, often quoting or referencing them in conversations. He kept a file on his computer called "Dad's Favorite Books, Movies, and Poems." The collection had hundreds on the list. The poem list was thin, but the movie list was extensive. He'd read anything from Stephen King to Shakespeare, Tolkien to Richard Bach.

"He did like to read," Chayton offered. "Remember when he had a discussion with that parent about people who looked down on fiction? He hated when people said *Harry Potter* wasn't great literature."

"I think those people are snobs," she added. "Mom and Dad never liked that intellectual snobbery stuff. Really odd given that Dad went to Stanford and Mom went to UBC."

"He really loved *The Lord of the Rings*, didn't he? It was the first movie he ever took me to," Chay commented. "I was like three months old, and *The Two Towers* had just come out. I supposedly took a dump when the credits were rolling. He went to change my diaper, but his brother stopped him and said he couldn't go. So, Mom took me."

"John was sick then, wasn't he?" she asked.

"Yes. He'd just been diagnosed. Let's not talk about that right now."

"Okay. Sorry. I never got to meet Uncle John. I have to say though that this book is kind of boring in how it is written. I'm glad they made the movies." She chuckled, but then her smile faded. "I'd give anything to have Mom and Dad here now and for us to be watching a movie. I just want a little bit of normal in our lives, Chay."

He knew exactly what his dad would say in response to the idea of normal. He would have recalled the shoot-out at the OK Corral in the Western movie *Tombstone* with Val Kilmer as Doc Holliday and Kurt Russell as Wyatt Earp. Doc was lying on his deathbed and playing cards with Wyatt when he asked Wyatt what he wanted out of life.

Wyatt responded that he just wanted to live a normal life. To which Doc said that there was no such thing as a normal life. Just life.

Chayton heard his dad's voice in his head. *Life under any circumstance is precious, and everyone—no matter how rich or poor—goes through the same process: birth, life, and death. The beginning and the end are the same.*

But the part in the middle varies. No one ever leads a similar or normal life.

All right, Dad, Chayton thought. *Maybe Doc wasn't contemplating the end of humanity, but I get your point.*

Chayton and Chenoa ate papaya and cold fried rice while sitting on the porch steps. Machi sat at their feet, nosing about for dropped crumbs. Kubi darted by as he chased a terrified lizard.

"They don't have a clue, do they?" she blurted out.

"Who?" he replied.

"The dogs. Do you think they have any idea about what has happened? I mean, look! They still eat crumbs and chase reptiles."

"I know they miss Mom. Not sure they miss Dad so much," he replied.

"He loved them. He just didn't think dogs should be all over the furniture," she defended.

"He was probably right. We just didn't want to admit it—him being right. He was annoying when he was..."

"He was annoying when he was wrong!" she cut in.

They laughed at this truth. They loved their dad, but his *patterns*, as their parents referred to them, could be trying.

"Do you think they know, Chay?" Chenoa asked, bringing the discussion back to the animals.

"The animals are definitely happier with fewer people to mess things up. They are free now, not locked up in pens while waiting to be slaughtered and eaten, and they can roam as they once did. But I think pets that had nice owners are sad. I know our dogs miss Mom. A lot. Kubi sits in front of her room every day. I think he is waiting for her to come back."

"Why'd he do it?" she asked.

"Who?"

"God. Why'd he do all of this?"

"I didn't know you believed in God," he sneered.

"I don't. I mean, I might. I'm not sure. I think there is *something*. Don't you?"

"Yes. I do. I feel Mom and Dad."

He then stood and spoke in a deep, resonant voice while throwing his hands outward.

"Children, I am God. Congratulations on making it this far in the game of Life. Now there are just two of you left alone with a bunch of wild animals, some of which want to eat you. I'd suggest reading some of my greatest works—either the Bible, the Koran, or the Bhagavad Gita—but at this stage, I'm not sure any of that will help. You can't really covet thy neighbor's wife when there aren't any neighbors. So, you're screwed, and I'm off to deal with other issues in the universe. Good luck!"

She laughed. "Pretty good impersonation, Chay. He sounded a lot like Gandalf."

"Gandalf is about as godly as I can imagine," he professed.

Chenoa washed the dishes and grabbed the orange dry mop from the laundry room. She wiped the floors, picking up layers of dog hair that had accumulated over the past few weeks. Her brother joined her, cleaning the windows and putting scattered items back in place. They'd been doing their laundry by hand and letting it hang out to dry. He collected their bedsheets and threw them into the large laundry sink to soak. They found comfort in this routine.

Their dad would have been proud of them.

Their mom would have chuckled.

Chayton walked down the driveway, carrying a bucket of fallen fruit that he had collected from their garden. He exited the driveway gate and turned left to the farm next door. Kuma pranced by his side. Piki lay next to the pen and raised his head as the boy and the dog approached.

Chayton threw grass to the cows and fruit to the pigs. The animals no longer ran to the back of the pen when the children approached. They were calm, less anxious. The children hadn't eaten the cows or the pigs, but they felt better knowing they had some food just in case.

He milked the cows. The milk was not the ultra-white, pasteurized milk they'd drunk for years. It smelled earthy and tasted creamier and sweeter. He also collected large white eggs from the chicken coop. These were much larger than before with more orange yolks and less runny egg whites. The children fed the extra eggs to the dogs, along with chicken mixed with pumpkin.

Chayton gently coaxed one chicken into his arms. He carried it back to the house and whispered a small prayer that he had learned from the cook at Green School. With a quick movement, he slit the chicken's throat and let tears fall down his cheeks. He cried each time he took a chicken's life, but they needed food for the dogs, and they felt better eating chicken and fish from the pond.

They had been raised vegans before moving to Bali. Their parent's expectations were that Bali would be a paradise for vegetarians. The Balinese, however, use a lot of tempeh and tofu for meat substitutes, which didn't sit well with them. Their dad had lost weight and was sick often that first year. The added heat and humidity took its toll on him.

"Chenoa, here are some chickens. I'll check on the scooters and the generator," Chayton said as he walked toward the garage.

He started the four scooters and the truck and let them run for a few minutes. It was just a precaution. They knew the bikes might fail at some point, but they didn't have the skills to repair them. He then walked outside and made his way along the paved stone roadway and to the main road. Piki darted out from a bush and joined him.

"Good boy. You are always looking out, aren't you?"

Four cars were parked in a row along the street across from the driveway: two Toyota trucks, a Toyota Avanza, and a Honda CR-V. The vehicles had been abandoned along the roads with their keys in them. Each truck carried two full diesel containers in their beds. He kept the containers outside until they drove to prevent fumes from building up inside the cars.

Petrol wasn't an issue. They stored hundreds of liters that they had collected from the service stations in their garage. He started each vehicle and let them run for a few minutes. As he did so, he explored a local food shop and found some instant noodles that Chenoa loved. He turned off the ignitions and left the keys in them.

No one but monkeys around to steal anything, he thought. *Might not be that long before we see one of them driving.*

"Come on, boy," he said to Piki. "Let's go back."

As he passed the toolshed, he wondered about the generator. He stopped and pushed open the wooden door, and a resting gecko flopped onto the floor. Piki chased it out into a bush. The windows offered enough light for him to make his way to the back. He pressed the generator's start button. The engine turned but didn't catch.

"Goddamnit. I should have run this thing. Come on." He pushed the starter again, but it wouldn't turn on. He then remembered how it had run out of diesel on the first day. He grabbed a container and filled the tank. After he tried the button again, the generator roared to life. He turned off the scooters and the truck he had left running and headed into the house.

Music blared. Chenoa sang and danced to "Thunderstruck" from AC/DC as it played from her phone and a Bluetooth speaker.

"We have power!" she screamed over the guitars.

"It will run until the fuel runs out," he said. "Maybe we can run it once a week to charge some things. I'm not sure how long it is going to last."

They plugged in their phones and the other speakers as well as their laptops. They also checked their phones for signals, but there were none.

"Let's have a movie night, Chay," she said afterward. "It is Sunday, our family day." She had kept a handwritten calendar since the event as something to do and to not lose track of time. She enjoyed using a pen and paper to track the days.

Chayton grilled some chicken with mango and made a salad from the garden. He had constructed a small fire pit out of stone and a metal grill in the backyard. Wood was plentiful, and they had bags of matchbooks since they had collected supplies from the Pepito market near Ubud. The store had reeked of rotting meat and fish, but there were ample dry goods and supplies that they had loaded into the truck and brought back home, including balsamic vinegar and olive oil.

He finished preparing dinner and took it back to the media room, where the family used to gather for movies and shows. Chenoa ran the air conditioner, which was a familiar comfort. She plugged her computer into the TV and started a downloaded episode of *Modern Family*. The strangeness was not lost on either of them, but they didn't care. They cuddled next to each other and enjoyed their food and the cool breeze blowing from the air conditioner as Phil performed the dance moves from *High School Musical* to his visibly pained children. They followed it up with a few episodes of *Ted Lasso* and *The Big Bang Theory*.

For a moment, a normal life had returned to Villa Jati. The children laughed, and the dogs chased lizards.

They fell asleep that evening with their heads at opposite ends of the couch and their feet touching in the middle. The generator ran out of diesel early in the morning, and the air conditioner fell silent.

Life returned to their new normal.

CHAPTER 7

THE RIVER

"WHAT ARE YOU doing?" Chenoa asked her brother on the back porch.

"Thinking," he responded, lying on his back beside Kuma.

"About what?" she asked as she squatted next to him, the sun reflecting off her blond hair.

"Why we are here. It doesn't make any sense. And why did the animals survive?"

"Maybe we aren't the only survivors."

"Are you ignorant? How many people have you seen over the past few months? Living, not dead. I think the answer is *zero*."

"Here? Yeah. But maybe people are alive in other parts of the world."

"Chenoa, you read the news that first day. Volcanoes erupted all around the world, and millions died. Maybe hundreds of millions. Billions. Dead. Gone."

"Okay, okay. I get it. Geez. Dad used to say, 'Without hope, we have nothing.' So, I like to have some hope."

"Well, I think he missed the boat on this one."

Chenoa knew this mood. She let him sit on his own since he was grumpy. He sat on the floor, rubbing Kuma's ears. She thought she heard him cry but knew this wasn't the time to ask.

Instead, she went into the kitchen to make a papaya and coconut salad for the both of them. She understood his frustration, but she knew being angry didn't help. Their dad would get angry at the most insignificant things at times. Usually, it was the dogs and the hair they left all over the house. Sometimes, it was the dishes left in the sink.

"Dad, you don't need to get so angry. It's not a big deal," she had said to him one time.

"I know," her dad had replied. "I just don't get why people can't do the dishes. It takes five minutes. It just bothers me."

"You can still tell people to do the dishes and not get frustrated. Mom tells you this all the time. It isn't good for your health."

He had smiled at her. "You are just like your mom. You see the world better than I do at times. Thanks for telling me. I'm still mad but thank you. I love you, Chenoa."

"I love you too, Dad."

She looked at Chayton sitting on the porch. She knew he was much more like their dad than her. After a moment, she brought the salad out to him. "Here you go, brother. A little treat."

"Thanks. I'm sorry. Who would've thought all those disaster movies we saw would come true? But even those used to have a few other survivors."

"I think about it all the time," she admitted. "Every night. We are alone, just the two of us. But I am glad we are at least together, Chay. And we have the dogs."

"Thanks, sister. You are so much like Mom."

She smiled.

The three dogs bounced off the side of the truck, antici-pating the walk.

"Sit!" Chenoa commanded them.

They continued to jump and bark, ignoring her commands.

"Jump in!"

They leaped onto the open tailgate and took their positions along the bench. Their feet rested on the edge of the truck bed, and their eyes strained to see ahead. She jumped into the back and attached the leash cara-biners to the metal clamp that sat in the center of the truck cab. Machi had jumped out once before when the leash was too long. Their mom had looked back to see her swinging along the side of the truck.

They used to drive the dogs down to the river a few times a week when their mom was around. She had to nudge and prod them, occasionally resorting to begs, bribes, and guilt trips. It was painful to get teenagers to do anything. Once they got to the river, however, they always had fun. The dogs would run into the water, swim to the island in the middle, and bark at the rafters float-ing by.

They hadn't walked the dogs since the event, as they now referred to the start of their new life after the disaster. It had been two hundred days since, according to Chenoa's calendar. As they came to the main road, Piki darted out from his compound like clockwork and chased the truck.

Chayton put the truck into four-wheel drive and drove down the steep, paved road. Bamboo and palms leaned across the road, creating a natural tunnel. They saw no garbage or plastic along the roadways. No dogs charged out of the compounds. He thought the animals must've abandoned their domestic dwellings as food was no longer provided. They did see a few dogs, but they watched the truck from a distance, slinking near the tree line. Monkeys and squirrels played in the trees, and birds speckled the branches. A herd of deer fed in the open grassy breaks.

"Chayton, deer!" Chenoa pointed. "They must be coming down from up north."

They drove down to an abandoned hotel that sat near the river's edge. The hotel had expanded from the river's opposite side before the pandemic since they had expected tourism to continue to grow. But the bamboo structures were now falling to the ground. Bamboo and alangalang roofs didn't fare well when left unattended.

The dogs strained their leashes. The children grabbed their bats, and Chayton strapped an Ace Hardware machete that he had found in the toolshed to his belt. The siblings let the dogs off their leashes, and the dogs bolted to the river along with Piki. The children followed but paused at the path above the river.

"I can't believe it, Chenoa..." he said.

The Ayung River was the largest and most sacred river in Bali. It flowed from the northern mountain lakes and winded down to the southern part of the island before dispensing into the ocean. It fed the nine-hundred-year-old Subak water system, the oldest active water irrigation system in the world. The Subak was a gravity-fed system managed by its own independent body that supplied water to all the Instagrammable rice fields across the island.

The Subak was life, and the Ayung River was its main artery.

But runoffs of pesticides, fertilizers, and pollutants had destroyed the river. Fabric and soda factories along it had devastated the ecosystem as they sucked out clean water and dispensed polluted runoff. Besides having some birds and monitor lizards, it had been devoid of life. Instead, river rafting companies were the life of the river. The siblings had rafted and swam in it many times before, but they would have never considered putting their heads into it, let alone drink the water.

But now, Chayton walked to the water's edge and stepped into the current. He ran his hand through the clear water and splashed it onto his face. Making a cup with his hands, he brought the water to his lips.

"Maybe don't do that, Chay," Chenoa warned, having not taken a step yet. "Are you sure it's okay?"

"It's clean, Chenoa. The river is *clean*."

"How do you know?" she asked.

"Because fish are *swimming* in it."

The water churned with activity as fish jumped and fed on an insect hatch. Not a piece of plastic could be seen, and a fresh, pleasant, musky smell filled the air. Turtles scattered the shorelines, and toads called to each other in an orchestrated cacophony. A hawk shot from the sky, hitting the water and flying away with a flopping fish. His mate watched from a giant fig tree, eyeing the river below as well. The hawk landed next to his mate, and they ripped into the fresh kill.

Chenoa stepped into the river and submerged her head. She threw her head back, and her hair whipped halfway down her back. Neither had cut their hair yet. And he noticed the definition in her arms and her muscular back.

Just downstream, a herd of elephants waded in the sandy bottom. A mother filled her trunk with water and playfully sprayed her baby. A large male rolled in the cool mud along the edge.

"Are those the elephants we released?" she asked.

"I think so. Yes. That's Swoosh!"

Kubi turned as something rustled near them. A pair of otters scampered through the grass. The female stopped, raised up on her haunches, and stared at the children. She glanced back, and three pups scurried toward her. The father darted into the water, returned with a river eel, and bit off its head. The pups fed on the wriggly delicacy.

"Look!" Chenoa pointed to a pair of Bali starlings flying overhead. "Where did they come from? There are never starlings down here."

"Maybe they came out of the Begawan Sanctuary up the river."

The Bali starling numbers had plummeted to only six birds left in the wild. The animals had been devastated as collectors would pay two thousand dollars a pair. The bird population had been brought back to normal numbers by Begawan, a foundation who collected birds from zoos around the world and bred them in captivity.

The starling pair landed at the river's edge and bathed in a soft current.

"They are so beautiful," Chenoa said. "I didn't think we'd ever see them in the wild like this."

"This doesn't feel like Bali, Chenoa," Chay admitted. "This feels like we are in a National Geographic episode."

The dogs chased the otters before settling down and playing in the water. The children, mesmerized by the new Bali, sat on a grassy knoll.

"Chayton, this is beautiful," she said. "I can't believe it. This looks like Pandora from that movie *Avatar*. All we need are some blue Na'vi to show up."

"This doesn't seem real to me either. I mean, it was green and pretty nice before. Everyone who had visited always said how beautiful Bali was. But that was nothing compared to this. Where did all of this come from?"

"Remember Mom talking about what had happened around the world during the lockdown with the virus? She showed us those videos of dolphins appearing in waterways in Italy and Turkey. Wolves and mountain lions moved into new territories in the US. Dugongs were in Thailand, and even wild boars walked the streets in Israel. Life was appearing out of nowhere simply because humans were forced inside. And that was a *short* period of time without human influence and consumption."

"I think it's pretty clear that humankind was kind of sucky when it came to nature."

They sat until the sun sank behind the trees. Neither wanted to leave. Chayton ended up building a small fire pit. The dogs sat quietly near them. The air was cool from the river and the valley, and the fire kept the bugs away. A calm settled over the river valley and the children. The fire crackled as the day creatures returned to their nests and burrows. They watched as the elephants made their way into the grassy fields and then disappeared into the tree line.

Afterward, the children loaded the dogs back into the truck and drove home.

"Amazing," she said.

"Amazing," he agreed.

CHAPTER 8

GONE

CHENOA LOADED THE dogs into the back of the truck and sat on the bench.

Chayton threw the daypacks into the back of the cab. "Chenoa, what did you pack in here? We're only going to the river for a day, not a week."

"We need food for us and the dogs, dufus. And I packed water. What have you done?"

"I have the fishing pole I found at our neighbor's house the other day. And I have a tent and sleeping bags if we want to spend the night. I mean, we have nowhere else to go these days!" he joked.

They no longer needed keys, nor did they worry about turning off the lights. But they did shut the doors and the gates just in case something decided to wander in from the forest.

"Remember that story about Dad and the chickens?" Chayton recalled as he slid the gate shut.

"You mean when the chicken and roosters wandered into the house, and he was just getting out of the pool, so he only had a towel wrapped around him?" she replied.

"Yeah. He tried to shoo them out of the house, but they scattered and ran. One ran to the back of the house and hid under my bed. Dad poked at it with a broom. It darted, and he chased it, jumping over the bed, losing his towel, and pursuing the bird naked." He laughed. "It left a trail of crap for Dad to run through."

"What a sight that must have been." She chuckled. "Thank god there weren't any CCTV cameras inside the house!"

They arrived at the same spot as the day before, near the dilapidated hotel along the river. Their three dogs leaped out of the car, and the children shouldered the packs.

"Chay, I think you need some new pants. You look like Huck Finn with his shin-length pants."

"When have we had time to shop, Chenoa?" he responded, placing emphasis on each syllable in her name. "What about you? Your pants are going up your butt crack."

"No, they aren't!" she countered as she reached back and pulled her pants down from her butt.

They had each grown a few inches and put on some muscle. She noticed that her brother was now the same size as their dad. She remembered seeing pictures of their dad when he had played water polo at Stanford. Chayton looked just like him but with a large mop of blond, curly hair rolling down his back.

The elephants lounged in the same spot as the day prior. The female turned her head when she noticed the children and the dogs. She flared her ears and raised her trunk as a welcome or a warning. Swoosh also waved his trunk in their direction.

Chenoa emptied the bag that had the tent poles and canvas. Kubi jumped on the canvas as it billowed in the wind.

"Knock it off, Kubi. Go play with Machi and Kuma," she directed.

He stared at her with wide eyes before turning to play with his companions. She finished setting up the tent and placed their bags inside. Chayton remade their firepit and placed a grill over a circle of rocks that he had built around the edge. He made a wood stack about a meter high near the fire and then fed the dogs rice and chicken.

He smiled at their work. It looked like an ad shot for Patagonia with their dark blue tent set against the forest and the running river. He grabbed the fishing pole and went to the river's edge.

His dad loved fishing. He had grown up fishing with his two brothers. His older brother was a talented fly fisherman, while the younger one was basically a professional. Chayton had seen the picture on his dad's computer where his younger brother had once fought a hundred-pound tarpon on a fly for over two hours. By the end, he had burn marks on his palm from the fish stripping the reel.

When they were younger in California, the brothers would get up at four a.m., bike to the reservoir in the dark, sneak in before it opened, and fish. They'd spend half their time avoiding the park rangers, sneaking around. But they'd always catch trout, bring them home, clean them, and grill them in butter for breakfast. Fishing bonded the brothers.

Chayton wished his dad was there with him now.

"Can I help?" his sister asked.

"Sure. Look for some grubs and worms."

She rolled over a rotting log to reveal a wriggling collection of worms and larvae. She put a handful into a cup. "Will this work?" she asked, handing him a flopping worm.

"I think so," he said.

He placed a bobber on the line, baited the hook with a worm, and cast it into the river. The line landed in the water, and the bait was taken by the current. In seconds, the rod tip thrust down. He jumped. Line stripped from the reel.

"Maybe that does something?" she said, pointing to the drag knob.

He turned it, and the stripping slowed. The fish, or whatever it was, pulled against the pole. Then a fish leaped as it got toward the shore, the sun reflecting off its gray-brown scales. He guided it toward the water's edge, lifted the rod, and flung it onto the grassy shore.

"Nice one, Chay!" his sister called. "Wow. I didn't think we'd catch anything."

"It's pretty cool. Never thought we'd catch a fish in this river. And look how big it is! Not like those scrappy fish we used to see in the restaurants. I think it is a tilapia."

"Does it just keep flopping?" she asked.

"No. I think I need to hit it on the head to kill it. You want to do it?"

"No!" She grimaced at the thought of killing the fish but understood it was a part of her new reality.

Kubi came over and licked the fish, but she chased him away. Chayton picked the fish up, turned his back toward her, and clubbed it with a piece of wood. He cut off its head, gutted it, and threw the scraps to the dogs.

Chenoa took her turn. They caught five more fish. The otter family appeared, curious of the commotion and attracted by the fish. He threw one to the family. The father grabbed the fish, and the family shared the meal. They wrapped the other fish in banana leaves and covered them with sticks until they were ready to cook.

Until dinner, they explored the river. The dogs bounded ahead of them. Down a ways, a dam spanned forty meters across the river. Dams were designed to manage the river by subverting water to the farmers and the Subak water system. The floodgate had been jarred loose, most likely by a fallen tree.

Chayton ran to where the dam connected to the shore. Trees had ripped through the entire middle section, and water flowed freely. *The dam will be gone in a few months*, he thought. *The river washed away humans' blemishes.*

A water temple sat just back from the water's edge, nestled against the tree line. The dogs ran into the ponds to quench their thirst. The children usually did not let the dogs near the temple since it was for sacred ritual, but now they waded into the crystalline water that was fed by a spring and swam. Chayton drank from the rocky outcropping that fed the spring.

"What are you doing?!" Chenoa yelled.

"Drinking."

"Yeah. I see that. But you shouldn't do that. You may get sick."

"Che-no-a," he responded, enunciating each syllable firmly. "The water is fine. No people, no pigs, no cows, and no chemicals. It's been running clean for months. It's fine. Besides, it's tasty. And we drank river water yesterday. This is cleaner."

She waded into the running water, cupped her hands, and drank. The water was crisp and cold. "That is delicious."

They played and floated in the water with the dogs. Hopefully, the Hindu gods would be understanding. But the dogs got tired and started back toward camp. The children followed, smiling and joking.

The fish sizzled on the grill, spreading a smoky plume. Piki joined the three dogs. They sat near the fire, awaiting dinner. Chenoa rolled out a blanket and placed mango and papaya in the center, along with vegetable rice. Chayton removed the fish and cooled them on a plate. Kubi could no longer resist the smell and grabbed the top fish, creating a charge by the other dogs. She yelled at them, but they grabbed their food and ate, looking sheepishly at the children as they devoured their meal.

The children ate the fish and fruit on banana leaves with their fingers. They were wholly accustomed to eating with their hands, given their time in Bali. Their dad's mom had been shocked one year when they had visited her in California. Forks, knives, and spoons sat on either side of the children's plates, but they ignored them and proceeded to eat with their hands. Their grandma hadn't been sure what she was witnessing, but their dad had explained that it was how people ate in Indonesia. He still asked the kids to use utensils though. They had complied but gave their grandma a despondent look.

The sun settled behind the trees. Darkness wouldn't come for two more hours, but the air cooled, and a breeze moved through the valley. Chayton threw sticks into the river for Kuma to retrieve, while Machi and Piki lounged next to Chenoa. Kubi chased dragonflies. He often operated to his own beat, oblivious to the world. Chayton and his dad sometimes called him Lenny, after a character from the novel *Of Mice and Men*.

Chayton threw another stick, and Kuma swam after it. She grabbed it in her mouth and tried to swim back to shore. But as the current pushed, she struggled, and her head dipped under the water. A rapid pulled her, and she couldn't swim free. Hopping from rock to rock that bulged out of the current, he made his way over, just below her.

He extended his hand, and Kuma changed course to flow downstream toward him. She arrived at the rock, scrambling for her footing. He pulled her up by her collar and held the shaking dog.

"Are you okay, Chay?!" Chenoa called. "Do you need help?"

"No, I'm okay. She's just tired and a little scared. We'll sit for a bit."

"Let me know if you need my help. The river is pretty fast today."

She watched them from her seat near the camp. Kuma had her head in Chayton's lap, and he rubbed her belly. Her breathing slowed down, and her energy returned. He looked off into the distance.

"Whatcha thinking about, Chay?" Chenoa called.

"Mm, not much. Wouldn't it be nice if Mom and Dad were here? Mom would be loving this with the dogs, and Dad would be out swimming in the river and fishing. Just kind of sucks. Makes me mad and sad and a bunch of stuff."

"I know. I know. It's all so depressing." A tear slipped down her face. "But this is a nice day."

"It is, Chenoa." He smiled. "It is a nice day."

She knelt and pulled Machi toward her. The dog licked the tears from her face.

"Hey, Chenoa!" Chayton called to change the mood he had created. He danced up and down the rock, gyrating his hips and waving his arms as he made a boom-boom nightclub beat.

Kuma jumped and barked next to him on the small rock.

She giggled. "You're a fool!"

She looked fondly at her brother and smiled. She opened her mouth to tell him that she loved him but stopped. Instead, she stood and danced. Machi and Kubi barked next to her. Piki sat like the Great Sphinx of Giza, still and with attitude.

"Nice one, Chenoa!" Chay called.

Kuma barked and jumped on the rock with him. The noise caught the attention of monkeys in the trees.

"Chenoa!" he called. "Watch—"

His foot slipped, and he fell, slamming his head onto the rock. He slid into the rapids, the river dragging him away.

"Chayton!" she yelled, running alongside him from the shore. "Chayton!"

Kuma barked from the rock. The other dogs followed Chenoa as she ran along the river's edge, trying to catch up to him. He waved his arm. She saw the panic on his face and blood streaming down his forehead. He mouthed words, but nothing came out. He then sank below the water and reappeared a few meters downstream.

"Chayton! Chayton!" she screamed. "Oh god, please!"

Kuma leaped from the rock and paddled downstream after him.

She struggled to keep up as rocks and trees blocked her pursuit. "Chayton! No, no, no. Damn it! Chayton!"

She could only watch as he and Kuma disappeared around the bend.

CHAPTER 9

ALONE

CHENOA SANK INTO the riverbank's silky mud. Dirt covered her face as she wiped tears away with mud-covered hands. An engorged mosquito fed on her arm. She brushed it away, and the blood mixed with the dark mud. She mechanically swirled the crimson-black mix in a circle on her forearm.

She looked downstream where the river turned the bend. She had searched for hours but to no avail. Kubi and Machi had run further ahead of her, barking at the boy and the dog bobbing in the water. They returned with less bounce in their steps and their heads hung low.

She had lost track of time. Even the night creatures had gone to bed. At some point, she stood, pulling herself up from the muddy quagmire. She made no effort to wipe the mud from her body as she crawled into the tent and curled up. The two dogs lay next to her. Machi put her head across her neck.

Piki sat just outside the tent entrance.

She cried and cried. Machi licked away her tears. She waited for the girl to fall asleep before closing her eyes.

"*Chenoa.*"

"*Dad?*"

"*It's okay, boo. It's okay.*"

"*Don't call me boo, Dad. I've told you that before. And you aren't even here right now.*"

"*I'm so sorry, little one.*"

"YOU AREN'T HERE. CHAYTON IS DEAD. GO AWAY!"

"*Dad?*"

"*Yes.*"

"*I'm sorry. I didn't mean to yell at you. Are you okay?*"

"*We are fine, Chenoa. Mom is fine; I am fine.*"

"*Where are you?*"

"*Here.*"

"*I'm not in the mood for your games, Dad. You and Mom are gone. Everyone is dead. It was just me and Chayton,*" *and now he is also dead. Kuma is dead. I don't need any riddles. I hate you all for leaving me. Just talk to me. Where are you?"*

"I am here right now with you. I've always been here with you. But I know this doesn't make much sense. Do you remember when Chayton found out about Santa?"

"Didn't you tell him?"

"It was late one night, and he was lying in bed. Mom said that he had asked if Santa was real. She didn't know what to say to him. So, I sat next to him. He asked if Santa was real again. I said he is, and he isn't. And I asked if he still believed in him. He said yes. So, I said that he is real then. He cried as his world had been turned upside down. Then he asked about the Easter Bunny and the Tooth Fairy, so it got a bit worse before it got better. But the point is that reality can be what you believe to be true."

"But I want you all next to me here, so I can hug you, Dad. I just want someone to hold me."

"You weren't always a hugger."

"Well, I am now."

"I'm giving you a hug right now. I love you, Chenoa."

"I feel it, Dad. Is Mom there too?"

"She is hugging you as well."

"I feel you both. Thank you."

"I saw you two down by the river with the elephants. You seemed happy then."

"Dad, it was so amazing. Can you believe there are elephants in the river? And did you see Chayton catch those fish?! The world is so different. I hate to say it, but I think the animals and plants are happier. They are growing all over the place. The water and air is clean. Buildings are crumbling into the earth. But the world is more beautiful. I just wish we didn't have to get rid of everyone to see all of this."

"Time is a funny thing, Chenoa. We liked to think that being around for eighty years was such a long time. Humans are strange creatures in that way. But each person's life is just a tiny blip in the span of the universe. Yet that doesn't make it meaningless. It is equally meaningful."

"But that's all we have, Dad. So, what more can we do?"

"That's right. It's all we have. And we spend so much time trying to be great that we forget about just doing good. We feel we need to accomplish things when we really just need to be. Look at the elephants yesterday. Do you think they are contemplating the meaning of life? Or are they just enjoying the river and the mud? Humans never really figure this out until it's too late."

"Well, it's too late for me, Dad. Everyone is gone, and I don't feel like swimming in a river alone or rolling *in mud like Louis Litt. I get the appeal, but not now. Maybe not ever. There was so much we were going to do together. You were going to teach me how to drive."*

"I did teach you. We rode scooters with each other."

"I meant a car. You taught Chay but not me."

"But I saw you driving, and you were doing pretty good. Chayton has taught you well."

"It isn't the same. It just isn't the same. I want you and Mom and Chayton back. I just want you back."

"I am here, boo. I am here."

"You don't get it. I'm so lonely, Dad. I'm so lonely."

"I know, little boo. But we're here."

"Hi, my luv."

"Mom?"

"Yes. How are you doing?"

"What do you think?!"

"I understand. I'm so sorry."

"Is Dad there?"

"Um... He's cleaning something."

"Really? He's still cleaning even when he's dead?"

"It's his weird way of showing love and helping."

"But he's DEAD! I mean, come on. What needs tidying wherever you are?"

"Things aren't so different here."

"Where's here? No, never mind. Forget about it. I'm not in the mood for this discussion again."

"Do you remember when we were building the villa there? You were around five years old. Dad asked you and Chay for ideas for the house. You wanted to make a birthday house that looked like a castle and had bright colors. Every day would be a birthday there. Dad thought it was so cute."

"Okay. So what? We didn't build a birthday house. And it was just a silly idea from when I was little."

"Dad didn't think it was a silly idea. And at the time, you thought it was the best idea in the world. You clearly imagined the house you wanted to live in, and Dad believed in your idea. If it wasn't for me, we probably would have ended up with a birthday house. But the point is that it was real to you even though it didn't physically exist."

"Dad wanted to build a hobbit house as well. It would have been fun to have a hobbit hole that we could climb into. I wish we had a hobbit house now. That would feel safer to me than sitting alone in this big house on top of the valley."

"You do have a hobbit house."

"Where?"

"The loft in your room. We built those as places for you and Chayton to hide and to be alone and cozy. Yours is quite beautiful with the crystals and the dreamcatcher and the comfy chairs. Maybe not a hobbit hole but pretty close."

"You are right. It is kind of like one. I never really thought of it like that."

"We both love you so much. Your dad loves you so much, which is why he was always doing those trips with you and Chay. His way of protecting you was to make sure you were safe and happy. No, you don't have an actual birthday house or a hobbit hole, but you have something maybe a little better."

"I feel better. Except the dogs can't get up the ladder to the loft."

"So, where we are isn't really much different from where you are. I actually think your dad is building a garden over there with some people. I'm not always sure what he is up to."

"I wanted a secret garden. Remember? We were going to build one in the backyard. But then all of this happened."

"You have one. It's just outside your room where Chayton made the forest."

"That ISN'T a secret garden, Mom. Jeez. You don't always get it. A secret garden has a secret entrance and a quiet space in the middle where you can hide and be protected. Chay just planted a big forest back there."

"Hmm..."

"Wait. It is a secret garden. How did I not see this before? Chay built a little path that leads to the center. There is a bench, and the forest has grown around it. It's like a cave, safe and protected. Oh, Mom. I love it. I miss you so much. I wish you were here to rub my head."

"I am, luv. I am here. Close your eyes and feel my hand stroking your hair."

"Thank you, Mom. Is Dad okay? Has he seen his brother?"

"Yes. They went fishing."

"Mom, what am I supposed to do? I can't do this alone."

"You aren't alone, Chenoa. You are surrounded by unconditional love. We are with you always. Remember we learned together that our souls chose to come and have this experience on earth and that we all have a purpose?"

"I remember, Mom. I just wish you were all here too."

"I know. Spread love to everything around you. Talk to the plants and animals and be grateful for them."

"I will, Mom, and I am. I feel more connected than ever to our dogs. Piki, Kubi and Machi are here with me. Strange. There are just four of us, like the four of us before."

"Maybe not, Chenoa. Maybe not. I love you so much."

"I love you, Mom."

"Dad?"

"Yes?"

"So, what should I do? I need someone here with me."

"I understand."

"Do you? You seem fine where you are. I'm not fine here. So, how do you understand?"

"Because I was there, and now I am here. And I can feel your feelings."

"Can you?"

"Yes. I feel your pain, sadness, anger, emptiness, and despair. It's okay to feel those things."

"No, it isn't because it's too much, Dad. It's too much. I can't do it anymore."

"What do you want to do?"

"Don't ask me that! You know how I feel. But what's the point anymore? Who cares if I am gone? Everyone is gone. Goddamnit! There is no point. There is being alone, and then there is being lonely."

"Yes, I understand. But what about Kubi, Piki, and Machi? Who will take care of them? And if it wasn't for you, the bears and the elephants would have died. You saved them all."

"They. Are. Animals! It isn't the same!"

"Is it? They have souls. Think about all the puppies you have helped and held in your life. You were like a mom to them. All we can do is care for what is living around us. And while it isn't the same with us here and you there, someday, we will all be together again. Remember that book I wrote—Drip's Drop—about the raindrop falling from the skies but eventually making it back to his family in the clouds? I believed that then when I wrote it, and now I know that is how life works."

"Will you sit with me for a while?"

"Of course. Do you remember when you used to sing on the back of the scooter with me? Why don't you sing a song? Those were some of my favorite times with you."

"I feel silly. But okay. I don't know which one. Can you pick one?"

"What about Both Sides, Now?"

"Which one, Dad? The Joni Mitchell version in *Love Actually* or the one from CODA?"

"Not sure it matters as you are the one singing it."

"Oh yeah. I'll try."

She mutters the lyrics at first but then gains confidence the more she sings.

"That is beautiful, Chenoa."

"Oh, Dad. I miss you and Mom."

"We love you, boo. We miss you too."

The dogs curled next to the girl in the tent. Kubi snuggled next to her back, and Machi wrapped her body around her head. Piki had moved just inside the opening. He rested his head on his paws but kept his eyes open.

A monkey howl broke the early morning silence.

The girl shifted and opened her eyes. "Oh, Chay..." she whispered.

Machi nuzzled closer.

CHAPTER 10

BEACH

CHENOA'S TUMMY GRUMBLED. She had no appetite, despite not eating since watching her brother die in the river. The thought made her wince, and she pushed at her temples with the palms of her hands. She knew this feeling would be with her forever. But she wasn't sure how long forever was going to be for her.

She decided to feed the dogs the food she had brought to the campsite the day before. Food splattered out as she threw it into the bowls and then dropped them onto the floor. Usually, they spread the dogs out when they feed them, so they didn't fight. But today, she couldn't care less.

She picked up a broom to sweep but quickly dropped it as she lost interest. The dogs wanted to play, but she pushed them away. She went to Chayton's room instead and sat on his bed. A notepad hung over the edge of his desk amid the clutter. She picked up the pad and read the scribbly handwriting.

Dear Mom and Dad,

I'm trying to do my best to take care of things. We are doing much better, but we still miss you. We are heading to the river tomorrow. Chenoa is more than my sister; she is my friend. I am not...

The words ended. He hadn't finished his letter. So, she imagined what his next sentence would've been: I am not ever going to leave her.

She stood, holding the pad and staring at his handwriting. Tears splattered across the page. She wiped them, and the ink smeared. She tried to dab at the water with his shirt that was draped across a chair, but that only made it worse. The paper and shirt fell to the floor as she crumpled onto the bed, sobbing.

Something wet wiped across her ear. She opened her eyes and met Machi's gaze.

"He's gone. What do I do now?"

Kubi jumped onto the bed next to her and wrestled with Machi. They rolled over her, and she pushed them away. Kubi jumped back and lowered his body into his playful attack mode. She smiled and jumped at him. He ran off the bed, followed by Machi.

She picked up the shirt and notepad from the floor and placed them on the desk. She stepped away but then turned back to his desk, placed the pens in the container, and stacked the papers. The notepad was now in the center with a pen across it. Maybe she would finish the letter for him someday.

She tried to find another place to be but felt claustrophobic. Wherever she sat, the house closed in on her.

So, she grabbed her backpack and threw in a water bottle and some snacks. She put on her black boots, cargo pants, and long red shirt. Her hair hung around her head like Cousin Itt's from *The Addams Family*, so she pushed it back and put on a Giants baseball cap.

"Come, Kubi and Machi. We're going for a ride."

They ran to the gate. She strapped a long knife to her side, grabbed a baseball bat, and headed to the truck. The dogs waited for her in the back bed, but she called for them to get into the cab with her. Machi sat in the passenger seat, and Kubi stood on the console.

She'd been practicing driving with Chayton but was still unsteady. The truck engine roared, but she let out the clutch too quickly, and it stalled.

"Damn it!"

She eased the clutch out more patiently and then gunned the car forward. It fishtailed up the moss-covered driveway. Piki sat up as they passed, seeming to want to come along. But she decided that two dogs were enough for one day. Maybe it was a good idea for him to stay around and guard the neighborhood. She then remembered that she didn't close the gates and regretted it.

Oh, well, she thought. *No people. Only animals.*

The diesel V6 roared down the road, breaking the island's silence. She drove with no destination in mind, wanting only to get away from the house and the memories of her brother. She *actually* wanted to get off the frigging planet, but that wasn't in the cards at the moment. Her sleep had been restless the night before, her parents' voices echoing in her head. She knew she was losing it and needed to distract herself from the grim reality that she was the only human survivor in the world.

"Where should we go?" she asked her dogs, but when they didn't answer, she continued. "How about Kuta? I'm sure that's got to be cheery these days. Although I can't imagine it without a few sunburnt Aussies drinking Bintang and proudly displaying their new tattoos." She chuckled. "Oh god. I'm turning into Dad by laughing at my own jokes. Well, he was pretty funny at times."

She recalled his joke about the two fishermen. They were having a good fishing day. One asked the other how they would find this place tomorrow. The other fisherman said to hand him a crayon from his bag. He took it and jumped into the water. After he came back out, the first fisherman asked what he had done.

"I put a big X on the bottom of the boat, so we can find it tomorrow when we come back!"

The first fisherman looked at him with disdain. "Are you ignorant? What if we don't get the same boat?"

Chenoa laughed. "Pretty funny, Dad. Pretty funny."

She looked out and noticed that the jungle was consuming the world. Villas and compounds had disappeared into the foliage; creeping vines had pulled plastic advertising banners into the underbrush. Plants threaded through shops. Monkeys perched on rooftops and took refuge in abandoned cafés. A large herd of deer wandered in the streets. She wondered if any lions were nearby.

An out-of-place male peacock strutted down the street, advertising with its fan-shaped train to females who might never come.

Mambal's market town typically bustled from the early morning with people balancing baskets on their heads as they did their shopping. The smell of durian and mango would permeate the streets. As did the stench of dead meat from the chickens and pigs. Self-appointed traffic managers would don fluorescent green vests that did little to improve the congestion as they blew their whistles and waved their arms to no one in particular. The children had passed through it each day on their way to school or to Astungkara Way, the organic farming program that their parents' friend ran.

While it now felt like an abandoned ghost town, this *new* town was also filled with life. Verdant green covered the cement buildings, and animals replaced the humans bustling in the streets. Within a year, Mambal would be a forest with a degraded pavement running through the center.

Chenoa slowly drove, avoiding cows, pigs, tree branches, and palm fronds. As she entered the main city of Denpasar, she slowed the car even more and shook her head in disbelief.

Denpasar had been a typical, poorly planned Asian city, much like Bangkok, Ho Chi Minh, Jakarta, and Kuala Lumpur. Main arteries were an afterthought, often with no consideration for flow or congestion. Inconsistent building fronts had lined the streets. A tangled mess of overloaded electrical wires had run between the buildings and the poles. Scooter drivers had pointlessly held their hands over their mouths to prevent inhaling the exhaust from aging diesel trucks.

Now Denpasar was an oasis.

A city of gray had become a city of green. Lush greens covered the dank cement. Red flowered vines wound about and covered the entangled electrical wires. A medium Bodhi tree had pushed up through a building, discarding the metal roof to the side. Flocks of birds moved in a choreographed flight, while monkeys played in the street. Even though it had only been less than a year since the event, some buildings were already crumbling and falling away.

Chenoa continued to slowly drive through Denpasar. She eventually passed the notorious Kerobokan Prison, which was made famous for housing drug traffickers called the Bali Nine and for the book *Hotel Kerobokan* that told the story of the prison's conditions. She shuddered as she considered how the prisoners met their fate after the eruptions. But perhaps they were in a better place now than before.

She then reached Kuta.

Frugal—mostly Australian—tourists would flock to Kuta for cheap beer, massages, affordable food and lodging, and parties. Kuta Cowboys, good-looking local men who wooed foreign women, would offer tours on the back of their bikes during the day and then a service at night. It was a game to them since they knew vulnerable people came to Bali while seeking love and change. Sometimes, they'd overstep what was already questionable behavior by trying to engage with teen girls. That had led to more than one confrontation on the beach.

Each night, Kuta had turned into a drunken fest. The government had allowed this behavior up to a point but arrested foreigners who violated temple dress codes or urinated in local fountains. As the evenings got later, and the people became drunker, women's attire would get skimpier, often offending the local populace. It was a peculiar game of wanting tourism money but also wanting people to respect the local culture.

Chenoa drove along the beachfront, passing a Hard Rock Cafe and a Starbucks. The emptiness was a somber reminder of her situation. She drove down to the

Beachwalk Shopping Center and parked in the middle of the street. She then got out and let the dogs run.

Looking up and down the long, wide beachfront road, she noticed that the windblown sand and sea air seemed to have cleansed the usual dirty sidewalks and roads. Lapping waves and rustling palms replaced the excruciating noise from unmuffled bikes. Seagulls and terns glided along the beachfront. The wind carried the salty ocean scent to her. A distracting smell. There was no more smoke or sewer odors. Instead, the ocean had now taken on a new aroma, and the air was rich with salt and seaweed.

It was pure.

As she stepped through the entrance gate, she raised her hands to her eyes to shade them against the brightness of the glistening white beach. The beach looked as if it had been bleached. There were no signs of plastic or cigarette butts. Bali beaches had been some of the most littered beaches in the world. Even Kelly Slater, a famous surfer, had complained about Bali's garbage and water quality, saying it was some of the worst pollution he had ever seen. He would have loved to see Bali now.

Kubi and Machi charged toward the water. Chenoa called for them to stop, but they were distracted by the activity on the beach. Thousands of baby turtles scurried about the sand, making their way out to the ocean. A few large turtles lay, warming on the beach. She ran to the dogs while gingerly stepping through the maze of movement. Kubi nosed one of the baby creatures but kept a friendly distance.

She plopped down, mouth agape. A tear fell down her cheek. She put her head in her hands and cried. Machi came over and nuzzled her. But she cried and cried, partly out of joy for seeing the thriving babies and partly out of deep sadness for being the only person to witness this miracle.

If only Chayton was here, she thought.

And she cried some more.

Kubi licked her face and jumped back into a lowered stance, wanting to play.

"Okay, Kubi. Let's play."

The dogs ran to the water's edge, careful to avoid the little commuters. Kubi bolted into the water, and Machi followed. They charged up and down the foamy edge, chasing each other into the surf and then up onto the white sands. Chenoa stripped down to her underwear and shirt. She jogged toward the water, calling to the dogs. They bolted after her.

She treaded carefully, not wanting to step on the turtles, and then dived into an oncoming wave. The salt water washed over her body, soothing her aches and diminishing her sadness. She dived down into the water, and while she didn't have any goggles, she saw flashes of fish darting all about her.

She stood in the chest-high water. Thousands and thousands of multicolored fish glittered in the sunlight. She leaned over and floated on her back, the Mother Sea gently rocking her back and forth. Time stopped as a peaceful presence spread throughout her body. She floated with the clouds, lost in time and space. She stared into the deep blue sky until something tickled her stomach. A baby turtle had crawled up onto her belly and rested under the warming sun. She continued to float, feeling the comfort of the natural world about her.

Kubi and Machi barked for her attention from the shore. She lifted her head, and her little friend scurried off her belly. After she swam to the shore, the dogs jumped on her. She wasn't sure how long she had been lying out in the water. The sun had shifted a few degrees down toward the horizon.

But she didn't want to leave the beach and the lapping waves. For the first time since the event, she felt loved and cared for. It wasn't the usual human connection she was accustomed to, but there was a familiarity. The sand supported her, and the waves spoke to her. The wind hugged her, and the sun soothed her. Mother Earth held her in her arms, protecting and caring for her.

She didn't feel alone.

She fell back onto the warm sand, staring up into the pillowy white clouds. The dogs settled next to her. She fell asleep, only to awaken as the sun started to set. The dogs had not moved. She brushed the sand off her body, put her clothes back on, and sat back down to watch the sky transition. She had sat on the same coastline, watching the sunsets, for years. Friends had always expressed how they had never seen anything as beautiful as a Bali sunset.

If only they could see it through her eyes now.

A pod of dolphins swam just offshore, leaping in and out of the water. There was movement behind the pod, much larger and in unison. A humpback whale surfaced, followed by other whales. Whales were common in Indonesia, but larger whales had never appeared along the southern coasts. The whale dived, flipping its tail. Moments later, the massive beast breached again, blocking the orange and red sun. It crashed into the water, sending a spray into the air that the sun painted as a rainbow. A baby followed just after, breaching in front of its mom.

Pure white beaches. Pristine water. Clean air.

Turtles. Dolphins. Whales.

Chenoa cried as the dogs sat quietly. The sun settled into the horizon, winking at her.

CHAPTER 11

THE HUNT

CHENOA SQUATTED BY the edge of the infinity pool that over-looked the valley. She felt cleansed by the ocean from the day before. The sun, the waves, and the turtles pushed off her sadness and anxiety. Her despair had returned, however, as she had rolled out of bed that morning.

Everyone was dead. Her brother, the only other person on Earth, was gone. She was alone, except for her dogs and the wildlife. She ate, slept, shit, and ate. This was not a life.

She despised this life. She glared across the valley, hating everyone and everything. Except there was no one anymore. She had no one to blame, no place to direct her anger at.

"FUCK!" she screamed and slammed her fist against the stone tiles. "FUCK! FUCK! FUCK!"

Machi and Kubi barked. They whined and tested the pool's water-covered ledge with their paws. They never trusted the illusion.

Her hand throbbed as blood dripped from her knuckles. The pain comforted her somehow. But the blood reminded her that she hadn't fed the dogs. Then she remembered that she hadn't eaten herself.

Vegetables, fruit, and rice weren't appealing to her and wouldn't be enough for the dogs. *I can kill a chicken. Or a pig?* But while the farm animals were there to provide food, she couldn't bring it upon herself to kill the only animals close to her besides her dogs. *My dogs. Not even our dogs anymore. I'm now down to one stupid pronoun.*

Blood rushed to her head as she quickly stood. She had to balance on the ledge for a moment. She wiped the blood from her hand across the chest of her white shirt, which reminded her of Native warpaint. She paused, staring at the streak. She then mirrored it in the other direction with her bloody hand, creating a wide inverted V.

She swiped her hand from the bridge of her nose to her jawbone, thrust her clenched fists down by her sides, raised her head, and gave the sky a bloodcurdling scream.

Chenoa put her black boots and long black pants on. She didn't change out of the blood-marked shirt. She tied a machete and the Swiss Army knife that her dad had given to her around her waist and stomped to the generator room across the yard. A long bamboo pole with a metal spike leaned against the corner of the room. It had been used for picking up trash in the village. But it was also solid, balanced, and evenly weighted. It would make for a good spear.

Machi and Kubi kept their distance from her. Her eyes were a little less inviting. The gate groaned as she threw it open. A gecko leaped to safety. She started to close the gate but then stopped. She was tired of being afraid. If something really wanted to get in, it could just jump the walls. And if it wanted to deal with her current attitude, she was happy to oblige.

The dogs did not bolt ahead. They stood close to her, protective. Animals were always safer in a pack.

The forest sang with buzzing cicadas through the heavy air. Machi lifted her head and sniffed, staring into the jungle. Kubi followed, seeming to sense something in the deep forest.

"Come on," Chenoa said. "There is nothing there. Let's go."

They walked down the path and toward the river alongside each other.

Eyes followed them as they disappeared into the trees.

Black pigs roamed the island, trying to reestablish themselves as a valuable part of the ecosystem. They were indigenous to Bali. Up until the 1950s, they were the primary source of pork that was used for special occasions and ceremonies on the island. Europeans then introduced the larger pink pig, and farmers turned to them to make more money and to meet the tourist demand for babi guling. A few local farms continued to raise black pigs for specialty restaurants.

As Chenoa made her way toward the river where she knew they'd be, she recalled a class on pigs that ran at Green School. Students would raise a pig and then kill it at the end of the year. While this was shocking to some, the idea was to face the truth about human food consumption. The children were not forced to slaughter the pig, but for those who did, they took part in a ceremony to end the pig's life.

She had never eaten pig. Her dad and brother would occasionally have pork at a restaurant and would rarely cook bacon at home for a Sunday breakfast. She, on the other hand, had been repulsed by meat, especially pig meat. She and her mother would pass trucks hauling pigs in tight, steel cages and sneer at the drivers.

Yet today, she desired fresh meat. Perhaps it was something primal within her. Her world had been completely stripped away. There was nothing except her and the animals. Some had already tried to eat her. They didn't give a shit that she was nice. She was the food.

But so were they.

Black pigs drank from a spring that was near a river. Chenoa hiked down toward it. Her dad had told her once that fishing and hunting were patient sports that required silence and stealth. The dogs seemed to understand that as well. They moved with her in a line, staying low to the ground.

"Okay. Let's be quiet," she whispered. "I'm not sure what the hell I am doing, but we're going to get one of those pigs, and then we will have a meal tonight."

Her heart pounded, and her breathing wavered. She shook her head in disbelief that she was hunting. If her friends and family could only see her now, they'd be in for a surprise.

She slowly moved forward on her belly and peered over the edge, looking down at the spring. A family of black pigs fed and waded in the clear water. The rushing river provided ambient coverage.

What the hell do I do? she thought. *If Chay was here, he'd have some plan of attack. He wouldn't have waited and would have charged by now, so we'd probably be running after them at this stage.*

A deep sadness washed over her as she thought of Chay. She wiped her eyes and clenched her fists.

Piki, who had now joined them, sauntered out of the bush and slid next to Machi. The dogs weren't the best trained and ignored commands. But today, they sat quiet. She grabbed her spear and edged down the embankment. Kubi and Piki circled the pigs in opposite directions, much like lions stalking a deer. Machi stayed next to Chenoa.

She launched forward and charged down the hill. Kubi and Piki attacked. The pigs squealed and scattered. Her target was a medium-sized male. She moved toward it, and the three dogs closed in. She raised the spear and tensed her arm to throw. Water ran off its tusks as it charged. She raised the spear above her head and threw her weight forward, releasing the spear as it reached the end of her outstretched arm.

It glazed off the pig's back.

The pig lunged at her, and she turned to run. But a piercing squeal ripped through her ears. Piki had tackled the pig into the pond. She ran for her spear, charged at the boar, and thrust the spear into its neck. It screamed, shook its head, and stumbled forward before falling onto its side.

She moved to the boar's side, took out her knife, and slit its throat. She put her hand on its head as it closed its eyes and died. She sat next to it for quite some time. Sad yet satisfied. The dogs sat around her, quietly respecting the animal's death.

"Now what do I do?" she asked the dogs. "How do I clean this thing?"

She remembered watching a show where someone who lived off the grid in Alaska had just killed a deer and mentioned that they needed to bleed the animal out quickly. She winced as she slit the pig's belly and pulled out its innards. She gagged at the bloody entrails and the putrid smell. Pig blood covered her. The bloody, inverted V on her shirt now sat as a hat atop a red, misshapen house.

"This would be a great episode of *The Twilight Zone*," she said to the dogs. "Maybe Rod Serling is looking down on me right now and considering the script."

She dragged the pig over to the cool spring water and washed its insides. She removed the head to lessen the weight before attempting to put the pig on her shoulders, but its weight was still too heavy, and she couldn't lift it.

"No way are you *not* coming home with me after all of this!" she yelled. She got as low as she could and threw its front legs over her shoulders. She worked the rear legs over her other shoulder and pushed up with her legs as she let out a groan. After wavering for a moment, she started the trek back up the hill with the dogs following behind.

Eyes followed the bloody girl as she shuffled up to the road under the weight of her kill.

CHAPTER 12

STRIPES

BLOOD COVERED CHENOA.

Her back ached as she lumbered forward. The carcass still lay across her shoulders, the legs swaying back and forth like a twisted marionette. The dogs trotted ahead but looked back often to make sure they wouldn't lose their prize.

Luckily, the gate was still open. She struggled up the driveway, pushed the second gate open as she balanced on one leg, and then collapsed. The thirty-kilo boar rolled off her shoulders and onto the basketball court. Her arms were too weak to massage her knotted back and shoulders, so she rolled onto her back and swung a knee over each side to stretch her lumbar. Less than a year ago, she didn't even like touching the frozen chicken packages for the dogs. Now, she lugged dead animals around like Jeremiah Johnson.

"Jesus, what the hell am I doing? What the hell did I just *do*?!" She grimaced for saying *Jesus* since her grandpa wouldn't have approved. "Sorry about that, Grandpa. But holy shit that thing is heavy, and I *killed* it!"

She lay in the late afternoon sun, the heat soothing her throbbing body. Yet she was avoiding the task at hand: the pig needed to be butchered.

She fetched a saw, a rope, a hatchet, and a knife from the toolshed. The carcass lay in front of her, and a trickle of blood worked its way into the bushes. She felt for the pig, and *Charlotte's Web* played in the back of her mind. She questioned again whether she really needed to kill the animal. The conflict argued in her head as her body called for sustenance beyond plants.

"I am sorry, my friend." She placed her hand on its shoulder, and tears trickled down her cheek. "Thank you. I know someday my body will go back to the earth. I hope it gives back to your family."

She recalled the Alaskan TV show again. She threw the rope over a beam that extended from the house and tied a rear leg to one end of it. She hoisted the animal to head height and then tied the other end of the rope to the other leg. The meat wouldn't last long, so she would cook it for tonight and attempt to smoke the rest. She knew she needed to skin the animal, so she used a sharpened knife to slice the hide away. A layer of fat separated the skin from the meat. It was both grotesque and satisfying to her.

"I'm like friggin' Wednesday Addams," she said and snapped her fingers twice.

She then whispered a quiet prayer in appreciation for the animal's life.

For a moment, she considered giving the entire carcass to the dogs. "I wasn't killing for fun," she told them. "I was hunting for survival."

She finished separating the skin from the animal and then cut it down the middle with a saw. As the first slab of ribs fell, *The Flintstones* theme song and the scene where a large plate of ribs was placed in front of Fred came to her mind. She hummed the tune as she washed the meat with a hose and threw pieces of excess fat to the dogs. She cut off the legs and gave one to each dog, who looked upon her with wide eyes, wagging tails, and lolling tongues. The three dogs took their feast and dispersed to different corners of the yard. They ripped into the meat and gobbled down the flesh.

She wrapped the last leg in a large banana leaf to keep the flies away and then carried the two rib slabs with her to the poolside of the house to start a fire in the grill. The dogs grabbed their gnawed appendages and followed her. They settled down with their meat once again on the other side.

She stoked the fire, threw the rib slabs onto the grill, and then jumped into the pool. A pink cloud floated around her as the blood washed from her body and clothes. She removed her clothes, washed the blood and mud from them, and then tossed them onto the deck. The cool water comforted her cuts and bruises. The new pond felt more healing than the chlorine pool of the past. The water had a slight fish-turtle-plant-bird smell that felt more natural. Nature agreed with her as a pair of Bali starlings and kingfishers bathed near the edge. A turtle's head bobbed in the water next to her.

She got out of the pool and was taken aback by her reflection in the mirrored windows. She almost didn't recognize the tall, muscular person standing in front of her. Her hair hung down to the middle of her back. Nicks and scars from the rigorous lifestyle of the past year marked her body. She'd always been healthy and active, but this person never would have appeared if not for the events of the last year. She felt as if she was staring at a stranger.

She wrapped herself in a towel and headed inside to change before dinner. As she glanced back at the pool, she noticed the birds had left their perches. Machi looked up from her meatless bone and stared at the tree line.

A slight breeze swayed the limbs.

Chenoa didn't see the shadow hovering on one of the branches.

Chenoa slipped on a pair of jeans and a T-shirt and made her way back to the porch, where the dogs barked and growled. "Hey, stop it. You have more food than you know what to do with. Quit being so greedy. Machi—"

A shadow rose in her peripheral vision. The dogs turned toward the movement and formed a defensive line. The form stalked forward and came out into the early evening light. At first, she thought it was a large dog or perhaps a mother bear. But this creature was *larger*.

The tiger moved within twenty meters of the dogs and then paced back and forth along an imaginary line. It never took the dogs out of its sight. Deep, guttural growls emanated from the dogs, ones that she had never heard before. Saliva flew from their mouths as they bared their fangs.

The tiger charged and swiped at the dogs, but they dodged and held their ground.

"Get back!" Chenoa screamed at the dogs. *Is this how I die? Is this how the last person on Earth perishes? To a tiger from a zoo? This is it. The world is going back to the animals.* "No," she said. "No, no, no! NO!"

The tiger stared at her and lowered its head. She saw the muscles tense along its back as it prepared to jump.

Anger grew within her. Her hands stopped shaking as her breathing eased, and her mind cleared. "I'm not letting you kill me today." She moved toward the fire on her right and grabbed a piece of wood that still burned at one end. "YOU WILL NOT HURT US!" she screamed and charged forward.

The tiger darted back. It retreated, and the dogs chased. She swung the lit log back and forth as she moved forward. Piki lunged in front of her. The hair flared on his back. Kubi and Machi joined in on the attack.

"Go away! Go away!" She held the stick in two hands above her head and swept it back and forth. "This is our home!" Sparks flew from the wood.

Faced with an attacking pack, the tiger retreated and ran back to the deck and the benching.

"Stay!" she screamed at the dogs to stop them from pursuing the cat. She backed up with them and watched from the corner of the deck as the beast perched on the deck benching.

It raised its head and roared at the girl and the dogs.

"Yeah? Well, same to you, bitch!" she yelled back.

A chatty gecko broke the early evening silence with its clicks and chirps. Her legs were numb from squatting, but she didn't want to take her eyes off the tiger. She felt better with her enemy in front of her. If she lost sight of it, then how could she step back outside again while knowing it could be stalking her?

Smoke rose from the grill, and her stomach growled. Not wanting to go inside to get utensils, she stabbed a slab with her hunting knife and dropped it onto the decking. She cut herself a chunk of meat and ripped into it with her teeth. Grease dripped down her chin. But the tender, fatty substance energized her. She cut off another piece and ate while never taking her eyes off the tiger.

The dogs refused to move from their positions between her and the tiger, so she collected their pig bones and placed them in front of each. They cautiously gnawed at the bones while also keeping one eye on the tiger.

Chenoa and the tiger locked eyes. She wasn't angry at the beast anymore since its countenance seemed to have softened. It sniffed the air, and a pink tongue moved over its lips.

She realized that it was a foolish idea the instant it crossed her mind. But the world was basically one big foolish idea these days.

She set down her knife and the meat she was munching on. Leaning over, she grabbed the extra leg that she was saving for the dogs. She moved forward and told the dogs to stay. Kubi and Machi obeyed, but Piki refused to let her go ahead alone. The tiger raised its head but remained on the bench. She moved within ten meters of it and then threw the leg toward it. It paused at first. Then it lumbered down onto the deck, sniffed the meat, and grabbed it with its jaws. After returning to its position on the bench, it fed.

The dogs eased and relaxed onto the grass. The agreement settled the anxiety. Chenoa gave each dog a slice of the meat and then threw another chunk to Tigger, her name for the tiger. She ate and watched. The food made her sleepy, but she resisted closing her eyes, fearing to lose sight of the animal.

"Okay there, friend. So, what's next?" She sighed. "You have an entire island of food. I see deer, pigs, cows, and goats roaming around, and I can't imagine there are that many of you carnivores. So, why here? Why me?"

Tigger stared at her and then jumped down from its perch. It approached but stopped within a few meters. The dogs raised their heads but did not bark. The tiger flopped down onto the grass, rolled onto its side, stretched, and then proceeded to fall asleep.

Chenoa noticed that the tiger was a female. Maybe she had lost her family and was also alone. Living in a cage and being hand-fed for so many years changed one's structure. Even with claws and a jaw full of teeth, perhaps she felt alone and desperate.

The sun settled behind the house. The herons were returning home to the east, flying across the valley and disappearing over the hills. The dogs slept but stayed between the girl and the tiger. Tigger moved away, snuggled next to a palm tree, and slept.

Chenoa lounged in her chair, the grill's fire still giving off heat. After cutting herself one more rib, she moved the meat to the edge of the grill. She gnawed on the pig, staring off into the valley. The sounds of the river settled over her like a soft blanket. She slid into the chair and nodded off into a deep, comforting sleep.

Chenoa awoke to a pitch-black night. She sat up abruptly and reached for her knife, scanning the area for the tiger.

The fire had gone out, Tigger had moved back to the bench, and the dogs were still sleeping.

The deep night was still. No moon appeared in the sky, and no insects made any noise. She breathed in the clean air and listened to the flowing river. She was alone but not lonely. She found comfort in the dogs and her new friend—as long as Tigger didn't decide to eat her.

"This was your favorite time of day, Dad," she muttered. "You loved it when the world was quiet during the early mornings and the late nights. I understand why now. I just wish you were here."

She sensed a presence behind her, but she didn't move.

A voice whispered.

"Chenoa."

CHAPTER 13

SWOOSH

"CHAYTON!" CHENOA SCREAMED.

Her voice cut through the rushing river before he was pulled under the rapids. His head bobbed up, and he saw Kuma lunging into the water after him. The river pulled so great that he could not get his footing and struggled to aim his legs downstream to protect against oncoming rocks hidden under the surface. Blood ran down his face and blurred his vision. The last image of Chenoa's desperation haunted him.

The rapid river took him downstream and tossed him against some boulders. Kuma disappeared into the white water. A submerged tree branch tore at his leg. He screamed as his knee slammed into a rock. River water shot down his throat. He was thrown out into the abyss, slammed into a semi submerged boulder, and then blacked out.

Chayton coughed and spat up water, turning his head a bit to find Kuma right beside him. She tugged on his shirt with her teeth once more.

He smashed into a tree trunk in the middle of the river, his body bending around the obstruction. He secured his arms around the tree as Kuma made her way onto the bank. Blood dripped down his face, and his energy was slipping.

The tree moved, but he held on tight. It lifted toward the shore but then fell back into the water. It then lifted toward the shore again and fell once more. The tree eventually carried him to the bank, where he rolled off and passed out.

"Kuma?" Chayton asked, waking to a face full of licks.

The dog's body shook.

He rolled onto his side as a sharp pain shot through his chest. He carefully pushed himself up into a sitting position. His blue and abraded legs throbbed. A deep gash ran down his right shin. His shallow breathing eased the pain from hidden injuries, but a gentle press to his ribs sent a shock through his body.

He could not recall where he was or how he had gotten there. He was cold. Hungry.

He rolled forward to the water's edge and drank from the fast-flowing river. "Come here, girl. Where are we? Where's Chenoa?"

He looked up the river, straining to recall.

A bunch of bananas fell next to him. He looked up to find an elephant standing over him. Ignoring the elephant in the room, he reached for one of the bananas, ripped it open, and wolfed down the sweet fruit. He then devoured two more. His energy returned, but the pain remained.

He looked over and noticed a marking around the elephant's foot. He placed his hand on the scarred skin that was in the shape of a swoosh. "Hello, old friend."

The elephant's trunk swung forward and sniffed at his face. He rubbed the boy's cheek and playfully nudged him. Chayton shivered as a breeze swept through the valley. The sun was setting behind the hills, and the valley darkened.

He tried to push himself up more, but pain from his ribs shot through his body, and he cried out. Kuma came to his side and licked his face.

"I'm not sure how I'm going to get out of here, girl," he told her. "I can't walk, and I have no idea how long I've been lying here."

The elephant trumpeted. His family appeared from around the river bend and made their way toward them along a worn path. Swoosh laid his trunk behind the boy and pushed forward.

"Knock it off, Swoosh."

Swoosh wrapped his trunk around the boy and lifted him up. Chayton grabbed the trunk, balancing himself. The elephant started to journey up the inclined path. Chayton, too tired and pained to resist, just rested into the comforting hold and awaited where the elephant would carry him to.

Chayton bobbed on the trunk. He expected the sound of walking elephants to be a thumping collective, but they walked as quietly as cats, their large pads absorbing their weight.

The path flattened. Buildings appeared ahead, and a sign hung from a pushed aside gate:

Amandari guests and staff only. No entrance.

"You have got to be kidding me," he said to Swoosh. "Of the thousands of hotels in Bali, you pick the most expensive one on the island."

The Aman chain of hotels was one of the most exclusive ones in the world. Rooms were thousands of dollars each night and came with a private butler. He remembered his dad had mentioned that Obama had stayed there during his visit. The hotel was across the river and about over a kilometer down from their villa.

The herd wandered into the central courtyard and waded into the green and salty pool. Swoosh gently set Chayton down and also made his way into the pool.

Chayton managed to stand and shuffled forward. "I'm not sure the owners would approve of elephants in the pool, Kuma." He laughed but then grimaced from the pain. "We'll just have to put the tab on the Underhills," he added, referencing the movie *Fletch* with Chevy Chase.

Chayton and Kuma stepped into the hotel entrance lobby, which was covered in bird and bat shit. His stomach begged for food, so he looked around. A sign indicated the direction of the restaurant. Monkeys turned to examine the shuffling creature. They screamed, seeming surprised at the appearance of the boy. Kuma silenced them with a determined charge and bark.

The stench of mold and rot hit Chayton as he pushed through a door to go into the kitchen from the back of the restaurant. He didn't even consider opening the refrigerator, afraid something would walk out on its own.

He shuffled into the pantry at the rear. The room housed dried foods, canned sauces, pasta, and other less perishable items. An additional door to the back read "Wine Cellar," which he opened and looked into the dark cavern. He tried the light switch despite knowing the outcome. A solar flashlight hung just outside the door. He pulled it from its cradle and smiled as it worked. *Maybe we should have gone off oil a little sooner*, he thought.

He descended into a smell of must and cork that was not off-putting. The scent made him recall when his dad had taken him to the Napa wine country when he was little.

Thousands of bottles lined the shelves in the Amandari cellar. None of the names made any sense, but he came upon a 1992 Cabernet Sauvignon. He recognized the grape, and his dad had said that red wines could age well if stored properly. The name of the wine was Screaming Eagle. That sounded kind of cool. He grabbed a few bottles and went back up to the kitchen.

He lit the gas stove with matches he had found, and the blue flames flickered. Wincing against the pain, he dragged a large Balian water container over to the stove, removed the plastic cap, and poured water into the large pot. He boiled the water, drained the pasta, mixed in bottled Italian pesto sauce from the pantry, and placed the pasta into two colorful Gaya ceramic bowls that had been made by the local and expensive Italian ceramic store.

He uncorked the wine and poured himself a big glass. He didn't know much about wine, but his parents had explained how to identify and enjoy fine wine. He swirled the wine in the glass and noticed it had good legs, which meant something he couldn't remember. The bouquet was, using his parents' vocabulary, of black cherry, currant, spice, and toasty oak. He gave it a sophisticated sip, slurping it to bring out the full flavor. He then took a large gulp and forked pasta into his mouth.

He poured bottled water into Kuma's now empty pasta bowl. He recalled that wine was poisonous to dogs. *It's poisonous to humans as well*, he thought, *but we still drank it.*

He raised his glass to the still setting sun. "Here's to you, Mom and Dad. I hope you are together."

A tear ran down his cheek as he recalled the many times they had sat around the dinner table as a family. He regretted the times he had taken that for granted, wishing that he could sit with his whole family once again.

He was in pain, but the image of Chenoa sitting at home alone was worse.

He would get back to her.

Chayton rolled over in the bed to face an all-too-close panting Kuma. "Good morning, girl. Your breath smells like garlic. I'm not going to kiss you."

She licked his face and wagged her tail.

A monkey sat on a chair outside the villa where the boy and the dog had slept. Other monkeys played in the background. The herd of elephants was gone; they must have returned to the river to bathe and to feed in the adjoining grassy fields. But Swoosh had stayed behind, lounging in the cool pool water.

Chayton sat up, his ribs throbbing, but the soreness had subdued overnight by him sleeping in a soft bed. The bed was now covered in river mud and other bits from the unkempt lodgers. He could only faintly recall wandering into the suite after dinner the night before. He somehow had enough wit to remove the top cover as it was covered in gecko poop. Even though it had been untouched for over a year, the bed was remarkably clean and did not smell of mildew.

"I'm not paying for those sheets," he said. "And I'm definitely not paying for this room, Kuma. The service sucks."

He rolled out of bed and went into the kitchen. His clothes reeked of river muck and teen. So, he undressed, washed his clothes in the sink, and then hung them on the restaurant railing to dry. He poured the rest of the water over his head to remove the dirt and grime from his body. In one of the rooms, he found a hanging robe.

He discovered some papaya and mango trees with fresh fruit for breakfast. He also cooked more pasta and sauce.

His family had sat on this side of the valley many times before since a restaurant called The Sayan House was just next door. The view had been considered one of the most beautiful in Bali, which was why many of the top hotels lined the ridge. It had now changed in over a year. Thousands of birds filled the trees. The sounds of the river were clear with no competing human-made noise. The call of monkeys echoed around, and the trees swayed as they moved through the branches.

Yet it was the rice fields which Chayton noticed the most.

The UNESCO World Heritage Site rice fields adorned Instagram with their elongated terraced steps. They looked like theater bleacher seats filled with growing rice. People would travel from all over the world to visit them. Now the untamed grass grew in waves. Hundreds of trees and plants had sprouted in the once unhealthy and environmentally destructive monocrop fields. Typically, nothing grew in those fields except for rice. Now, the forest and the fields blended together. In a few years, the fields would be entirely gone.

The valley was rich and full, greener than ever before.

Chayton breathed in the trees. "I would give anything to have Mom and Dad back here, Kuma. I know I shouldn't be saying this, but humans really messed up the world. We all knew it, but we never really wanted to admit it. I wish I could film this and go back in time to show the world. But that ain't going to happen."

He put his head back to rest his exhausted body. Kuma lay next to him, checking often to ensure the boy was still breathing.

The sun moved beyond midday as a roar awakened Chayton.

"What was that?" he asked Kuma.

The roar came again from up the river valley.

He knew it had come from the direction of their villa. "I have to get back to Chenoa," he said as he stood.

He put on his still-damp clothes and limped forward to descend the path. His eyes searched for a walking stick to support him.

A raspy breath came from behind him, and he turned to find Swoosh standing and extending his trunk to the boy. He sat on his trunk. The elephant lifted him up to the top of his head, where he fell onto the massive back.

"So, you want to give me a ride? Okay. How do I drive? Go!" he commanded.

The elephant didn't budge.

"Straight!"

Nothing.

"Lurus!" he tried in Indonesian to indicate straight.

The elephant lumbered forward, and Kuma followed in the rear. Chayton winced each time the elephant stepped but smiled as he headed back to Chenoa.

He chuckled to himself and then yelled back in the direction of the hotel. "Make sure you put it on the Underhills!"

Kuma looked up and darted forward, wagging her tail. Swoosh followed.

The roar echoed once again.

CHAPTER 14

WHISPERS FROM THE PAST

"CHENOA," A VOICE whispered.

Stop it, she thought. *Why are you messing with me? I mean, come on. There is a frigging tiger in my yard. Leave me alone.*

"Chenoa."

"Go AWAY!" she yelled.

The dogs bolted upward, and the tiger raised her head.

"Chenoa," the voice came again.

She turned to yell at the whispering spirit but froze. The ghost appeared worn and weary, like Scrooge had stood in front of his own tombstone.

"Chayton? Chayton?! CHAYTON!" She rushed forward and wrapped her arms around her brother.

His arms hung at his sides. He smelled of the river and animals, and streaks of mud rolled down his face.

She extended her arms to look at him. He was *real*. She quickly pulled him back toward her again.

He rested his head on top of hers and exhaled. "Chenoa," he whispered. "Chenoa."

She eased him into the lounge chair and rushed to the kitchen for some coconut water. He gulped the drink down, most of it dribbling down his chin. He then pointed at the meat on the grill. She broke off a rib and handed it to him. She then noticed Kuma, who was sniffing her lost companions.

She handed some meat to her. "You are a good girl. Did you take care of Chayton?" She buried her face in the dog's neck, crying with happiness to have their family back together again.

The meat satisfied the hungry boy, and he pointed for more. But his hand froze midair as he noticed a nearby beast. "Chenoa, don't move... There's a tiger in our yard."

"I know."

He gave her a curious look. "What is a tiger doing in our yard?"

"I think she wanted to eat me, but we ended up just having dinner together. It's a long story."

"Oh, thank god. By the way, there's an elephant in the front."

Chenoa stoked the fire, and Chayton shared his story of the past few days, often stopping as she broke down crying. The realization of them being the last people on Earth hit home to them. They were not only the last of humanity but the last of their family. They felt more of a need to live for each other.

What would Spock have said about this? Chayton thought. *The needs of the many are more important than the needs of the few. But when the many and the few are gone, what now? Live long and prosper?*

He shook his head of his thoughts and turned his attention back to his sister and the meat she had given him. "So, where'd the pig meat come from?"

"I killed it," she said simply.

"Yeah right."

"No! I killed the pig. I tracked it down by the pond, and the dogs helped. To be honest, it's a bit of a blur, and it may not have ended well, but I killed it, hauled it, skinned it, and cooked it. That's when Tigger appeared."

"Tigger?"

"Yes, Tigger. She ate half the pig, which seems to have stopped her from wanting to eat me and the dogs. She's just been hanging out and napping over there." She paused for a moment. "So, you brought an elephant?"

"Oh yeah. Swoosh is in the front. He brought me here."

They sat as the morning light blessed the eastern sky. The dogs dozed around them, while Tigger lounged on the benching on the back deck.

"Dad struggled with the three dogs we rescued and brought home," Chenoa said. "Can you imagine if he came home now to see a tiger and an elephant in the yard?"

"I think he'd be okay with it, Chenoa." He smiled. "I think he'd be okay."

Chenoa awoke next to Chayton. She threw some ribs to the dogs and then paused to observe Tigger. A bird squalled. A *coucal*, she thought. Tigger stared into the valley, gently lifted her head to sniff the air, and then gave a lengthy moan. It was a haunting sound, almost a cry or a wanting.

"Is your family gone, girl?" Chenoa asked.

Tigger's eyes locked with hers. Neither blinked until the tiger turned back toward the valley.

"If they are there, I hope you find them. I understand how you feel."

She moaned an eerie call. No answer came from the valley.

"You can stay here, but please don't eat my brother. Okay?"

Tigger licked her lips and rested her head on her paws. The dogs remained between the tiger and the children.

Chenoa ran to their farm next door, passing the elephant along the way. Swoosh had trampled the living fence that surrounded their garden and was eating papayas from a tree.

"You just stay here on this side of the house for now," she called out. "Not sure you and the overgrown cat on the other side of the house will get along. I'll leave the gate open for you, so you can just leave when you're done."

She gathered eggs from the chicken coup and then caught and killed three chickens. Dozens of baby chicks trailed their mothers. She also collected some milk from a mothering cow. She returned to Swoosh to gather some papayas from where he was feeding. The elephant extended his trunk and brushed the girl's face. His skin was rough, but she embraced the trunk and pressed her cheek against it. The contact comforted her. The elephant rumbled and wound his trunk around her.

"Thank you for bringing my brother home," she said. "You take whatever you want from our garden." She hugged the trunk and said goodbye.

"Chay? Do you want to wake up?" Chenoa asked.

He rolled onto his side and sat up. She handed him a rib, a papaya, and milk. He wolfed the food down. She then cut up two of the chickens, fed one to the dogs, and placed the other on the grill to eat later.

With the third chicken, she approached Tigger. The dogs got up to move with her, but she commanded them to stay. She prepared to throw the chicken toward the cat but paused and decided to get a bit closer. She carefully walked onto the deck and moved forward. If the cat charged, she'd run into the pond and dive to the bottom. She waved the chicken in front of her, and the enormous Tigger sat up.

She second-guessed her decision. The cat moved forward and came within two meters of her. She presented the chicken. The tiger licked her lips and then gently took the bird. Tigger paused for a moment, her big eyes locking with the girl's, and then moved back to her corner of the deck.

Only as she moved away did Chenoa realize how fast and hard her heart was beating.

Nostalgia came over Chenoa as she repeated the tiger's name. *Tigger was from* Winnie-the-Pooh, she thought.

She recalled her dad's full name, Robin John Christopher Thompson. He was named after a friend of his parents' in the UK, whose name came from Pooh's friend. He had hated his first name growing up since people teased him for either being a bird or a sidekick. Why he and Mom named their kids after birds—a dove and a falcon—perplexed her.

It also explained why he grew up being called by his third name: Christopher.

She left her brother asleep and protected by the dogs as she meandered into the house. It felt distant to her.

She picked up the top copy of her dad's *Stanford Magazine* collection from the round table. Its edges curled, and she traced the coffee stain on the cover. She lifted the magazine up, pressed her face into the cover, and breathed in the smell, imagining a faint coffee scent left by her dad's cup.

A picture of three children—her mom, her mom's brother, and her mom's sister—was juxtaposed in a frame with them in formal attire at her parents' wedding. She spun the antique globe and watched as Asia, Africa, Europe, and North America rotated in front of her. Golden Buddhas that her mom had gotten in Singapore sat covered in dust, endlessly contemplating.

The living room opened into a hallway that led to the master bedroom. In the bedroom, Chenoa ran her hand over a wedding photo of her parents kissing. She turned back to the photo, staring at the couple. The characters became animated, turning and waving to her, and then returned to their original pose.

Dad's Montblanc watch that he had gotten from Mom in Japan sat on his bedside table with the date and time frozen. Chenoa had looked through the bedside drawer many times over the years, usually looking for loose change or a stray bill. She now rummaged to discover a worry stone, two teeth in a packet, and a bookmark with the inscription: "Reading forces you to be quiet in a world that no longer makes a place for that."

The green oval worry stone was cool to her touch and had a thumb-sized depression on one side. She ran her thumb back and forth over it, wondering how many times her dad had rubbed the stone. He had picked it up in Ireland when he had traveled there with his parents and his girlfriend. He often kept it in his pocket to offer comfort during times of stress. He could manage the most complicated situations in the workplace but often struggled with the little things that made his world feel out of control. He strove for a quiet mind and a peaceful heart. He had found them for the most part, but childhood patterns shaped from an alcoholic father had affected him.

She knew the small packet with her and Chayton's teeth was a reminder to him of the good things in life. The teeth were brown and ugly but getting rid of them had felt like getting rid of his kids. So, they had remained in his drawer, next to his diaries and journals.

She placed the items back in the drawer but slipped the worry stone into her pocket and gently rubbed it with her thumb.

A little Buddha stared at her from a corner across the room. It sat perched on her dad's desk. Its head was tarnished from her dad placing his hand on it each time he had sat to work or to write. The desk itself overlooked the pool and the valley. Her mom had created that work corner for him; she had always tried to make the house homier. Chenoa sat at the desk, remembering her dad sitting here and the times they had sat together.

A triangular piece of folded paper sat under a white crystal near the computer. The paper was for table-top football, which they would play in restaurants. She chuckled as she remembered them clearing the table, wiping it down, and then tapping the triangle back and forth to reach the opposite edge without it falling over. Then they'd flick it toward their opponent, who made a goalpost with their fingers, across the table. How often had the folded paper flown too far and landed on another table?

She pressed the button to turn on her dad's computer but then remembered there was no power when nothing happened. She headed to the generator room, passing Chayton sleeping on the couch. Tigger was absent. She panicked and scanned the yard, looking for the tiger. The dogs had not moved, so she assumed the cat had left down the back hill. The generator roared to life after a few tries.

The computer turned on, and the login screen appeared. How odd that the world before was protected by passwords and codes. The world had been secrets within secrets.

She typed in her dad's password, and the desktop background appeared. It was a picture of the four of them in Thailand at the Death Railway, which had been built by Allied prisoners of war during World War II.

"What are you doing?" Chayton asked from behind her.

She turned around to face him. "You were so tired that I just let you sleep. I'm glad the tiger didn't eat you."

"Yeah. Me too. So, what are you doing?"

"I turned on the generator and started up the computer. Remember this?" she asked, pointing to the picture of the four of them balancing on a rail track.

"That's part of the railway Mom's grandad built when he was a prisoner during World War II. There was even a movie about the same Death Railway, *The Bridge on the River Kwai*. Remember we saw the photo of him as a prisoner at that Thailand war museum?"

"People survive the worst human atrocities, and then nature commits the worst one."

"Not sure Mother Nature really meant it. I think stuff just happens," he said.

Changing the topic, she asked, "Remember Dad had files on Google Drive for us for when something happened? I want to see them."

"Here. Let me help." He walked toward her. "He showed me where everything is."

Their dad might have been the most organized person they had ever met. He might have been the most organized person in history in some ways. Everything had its place. His shirts, pants, and underwear were organized to rotate through on a regular basis. His email inbox never exceeded one hundred emails and was usually under fifty. When any family member had asked him for a document, he'd annoyingly remind them they all had access to the Drive.

"But we can't go online," Chenoa said. "How do we get them?"

"He had everything saved offline. He basically had a postapocalyptic management plan." Chayton laughed.

"What is that file?" She pointed to a folder called "Writing."

He opened it to discover all of his dad's writings and some unfinished projects. There was his children's book, *Drip's Drop*, and other projects he had done over the years. He opened a folder called "Butterfly."

"That's the novel he was working on, Chenoa," he said. "He had worked on it for over a year but never got to finish it. Makes me sad to think about. He always wanted to write a novel for us but never got to. I wish he had finished it. It would be nice to read it now."

They opened the family folder and found "Dad's Favorite Movies, Books, and Poems." It opened with a small introduction: "I hope you enjoy. Maybe as you read them, you will remember why I enjoyed them so much. I love you. Dad."

"There it is! *The Lord of the Rings*, his favorite book and film. How many times did he watch that damn movie?" Chenoa asked.

"He sure had a lot of things listed. Holy crap! He read a *lot* of books. He said he read every day, but I didn't know he read this much. Look at his top ten."

1. *The Lord of the Rings Trilogy*
2. *The Hobbit*
3. *The Count of Monte Cristo*
4. *Al-Anon's Twelve Steps and Twelve Traditions*
5. *The Overstory*
6. *Watership Down*
7. *Ethan Frome*
8. *A Sense of Wonder*
9. *Of Mice and Men*
10. *Where the Red Fern Grows*

"I don't think we did a great job reading, Chenoa. He and Mom were always a bit frustrated with us. But I wonder what the point would be to read any of these now when there isn't anyone around anymore to discuss them with."

"What about me?" she challenged.

"Yeah, yeah. There is you. I think we can read them. But reading was about learning life stories, studying history, and seeing how we can be better in our lives. That world is gone. Forever. What's the point if humanity ends with us?"

"So, what then is the point anymore? Do we just give up and die? Is there any value to books and history and all that? Why the hell do we talk then?"

"*Okay.* Take it down a notch, Homer. We don't have to worry about history repeating itself anymore." Chayton paused and sat back. He wasn't usually prone to over consideration. He said what he thought and followed his intuition.

She waited.

"I think the point of life was survival in some way, and that is still the point. And Dad and Mom used to talk about connections to ourselves and to others and to the world. Maybe that's it: continuing to connect with life. Just enjoying what we have. You. Me. The animals. The new world around us."

Chenoa looked at her brother with a bit of surprise. *Pretty wise words*, she thought. "Open the letters to us, Chay. He has a letter for you, me, and Mom."

He opened the letter to him, and he read some parts out loud.

My Dearest Chayton,

I write to you now as someday I may not be with you and Chenoa and Mom. That isn't my plan. But we can't always plan our lives as you will see as you get older...

Who knows when, if ever, you will read this? In a way, this is a backup to express my love to you as your dad in case you aren't old enough to remember me or perhaps you were too young to remember our times with each other. Of course, what I hope for the most is that I live to an old age with all three of you, and perhaps we will get to read this together at some point when you are older.

As I come home from work, my heart swells when I hear daddy come from your lips. Half the time, you are in the middle of a pillow fort, so I have to come find you, but the other half, you run to me and hug me.

There is so much to learn in life, but one thing I hope you learn is to just be yourself and be happy with yourself. Life is a struggle for everyone, and it has its ups and downs. Being true to yourself is the most important thing you can do. We will never tell you what you need to be when you grow up; we will only be there to guide you and to help you achieve your dreams.

You have given me a lifetime of joy and happiness, and I hope that I get to experience that with you for many more years ahead. But just in case, my very dear boy, I want you to know how much I love you. And whether or not I am with you physically, I will always be holding your hand and watching over you. Always.

I couldn't have asked for greater gifts in life than you and Chenoa. I was lucky to have met Mommy.

I love you, little buddy. I will always be by your side with my arm around you.

Love, Dad

They finished his letter, and then they read the letters to Chenoa and their mom, which shared similar sentiments. They sat, staring at the letters to each of them split on the screen. The letters were many pages in length, detailing times of their lives over the years. They sat quietly, not looking toward the other, with tears streaming down their faces.

Machi entered and nuzzled Chenoa. The girl moved to the floor and hugged her, burying her cries into her neck.

"Chenoa, look at this," Chayton said. "I think it is a poem written by Dad. It's called 'Oh Little Dove.' I think it is about you."

> *Oh, little dove, how you flitter and float.*
> *You dart about with songs from your throat.*
> *You're young of age, but wisdom reigns,*
> *As you see the world and all its pains.*
>
> *Perched on the chair, you observe and listen,*
> *But you're filled with ideas and want to hasten.*
> *Your wings go aflutter to get their attention.*
> *Sometimes, you are lost in the loud conversation.*

The wind blows hard; rain pours from the sky.
You don't budge; you are determined as I.
Yet the storm blows too hard and shakes your branch.
It might be time to let go of your stance.

A cage will never be your home.
You need the sky to fly and roam.
But each night you return to your nest,
And cuddle into your mommy's breast.

Oh, little dove, you are perfect and true.
You are loved and wanted as the sky is blue.
Flow with the wind, feel the freedom.
Know you are loved forever and some.

"He really loved you, Chenoa," her brother said.

"He loved all of us, Chay."

The screen saver started. A picture of their mom and dad kissing scrolled by, followed by images of the family through the years. Life captured in forty thousand photos in a library for the last two people.

Chayton reached out and touched the screen as a photo of their parents appeared. "I love you," he whispered.

"I miss you," came a voice from the floor.

She slid her hand into her pocket and rubbed her thumb against the stone.

CHAPTER 15

THE CALL OF THE COUCAL

A GREATER COUCAL perched in the durian tree above the dogs and the children. He watched the children play a failed game of frisbee with the dogs.

The bird was largely black with distinctive rust-colored wings and a heavy, long, black tail. His deep red eyes added to the bird's mythology as an omen, a harbinger of good fortune in Asian cultures. Yet his attention wasn't on the activity below him.

The bird called out a deep, resonant warning to the children below. The children turned to look at the bird, and a chill ran down their spines.

Omens weren't always good.

"Let's get out of here," Chayton said as he threw the frisbee over Chenoa's head and into a bush.

She frowned at his poor control as she searched the plants to retrieve the disk with Kubi. "Glad you are feeling better, Chay. What do you want to do?"

"While I could have skipped the river episode, it was kind of fun hanging out in the hotel. Why don't we pack a few things and find a villa along the road just for a change of scenery?"

"We have a nice villa. And food..."

"Yeah, yeah, yeah. I get it. But remember when Dad just liked to get away for the sake of getting away? Whenever he went somewhere, he came back refreshed and with a slightly different perspective. I felt the same at the hotel."

Chenoa knew she wasn't going to win this discussion. And in her heart, she was excited to spend a few nights away. She needed a change of scenery as well. So, they packed up the truck with some supplies and the dogs and headed south. She remembered a villa that sat fifteen minutes down the road. Her dad had spoken about it since he knew the owner. They turned off the main road and pulled into the parking area.

The villa sat on two hectares and spanned the river. It was composed of multiple traditional structures. The owner rented the entire property for twenty thousand dollars a day. The villa included a deck that extended over the river and a private bird sanctuary. The children performed a quick scan of the grounds, checking each villa to see if any corpses lurked in the shadows. The rooms were empty and, apart from some mildew, all in good shape.

They placed their bags in one of the rooms and explored the main joglo structure, which included an open kitchen, pantry, and ample seating. There were fresh water, gas tanks, and dried food in storage. They swept away the gecko and bat droppings and cleaned up the area. Outside of overgrown bushes and a few monkeys who had made the property their home, the facility was in very good shape and more than livable.

Chenoa noticed Chayton's hesitation as he prepared to jump off the decking and into the river. "You okay, brother?"

"It is weird to consider that I could have died in this river. Things happen so quickly in life. That's kind of a stupid thing to say given all that just happened the past year. But none of us are immune from when life decides to take us."

Chenoa knew this better than anyone. She had sat for days, believing her brother was lost forever. But she didn't want to think about it anymore. She kicked off her shoes and jumped into the river. Chayton and the dogs all followed.

They spent the day by the river and caught enough fish for dinner.

Only Piki did not participate in the activities. He sat erect with his ears perked, staring into the dense jungle across the river. A coucal called from the canopy.

The children spent two nights at the property, hiking, swimming, fishing, and enjoying their time with each other. On the third night, Chayton started a fire and barbequed the fish they had caught. The sun was setting, and the dogs awaited their dinner.

"I'll get some fruit and coconut water from the kitchen, Chay. You need anything?" He shook his head and continued to tend the fire. Chenoa smiled as she watched him prepare the food. He had changed since the river. He lost none of his jovial character, but he had grown up in many ways. She saw their dad in him.

A dog moved behind her as she searched the pantry for snacks.

"You just ate," she told the pup. "I'll get you more food in a bit."

"I'm not hungry," came a raspy, heavily accented female voice. "Don't you move, or I'll shoot you and your brother out there."

Chenoa turned to face the first person she had seen in two years. Elated, she ignored the gun and the sneering face and moved toward the figure with open arms.

"What are you doing, girl?" came a shrill and now distinguishable Australian accent. "I'm not your mother!"

She stopped, stricken between the overwhelming emotion of seeing another human and the threatening actions of the intruder. "Where did you come from? Are there others? We won't hurt you. We can help."

As she spoke, another person emerged from the back room: a middle-aged man of about the same age as his partner. "This little one has a damn mouth on her, Olivia," he said with an Australian accent.

"No kidding, Jack," she replied with a sneer. "She won't shut up."

"Move it, girl. Let's go outside," he said.

Chenoa slowly walked outside as the two intruders followed her. She tried not to make much noise. Saliva flew from the dogs' jaws as they charged the strangers.

She jumped between the dogs and the strangers, fearing they would shoot the animals. "Machi, Kuma, Kubi! Stop!"

Chayton looked up to see the strangers. He, as well, was more excited to see people than concerned about their threatening presence.

"Get those goddamn dogs to stop barking!" Jack yelled as he fired a shot over their heads. "I'll shoot 'em if they don't shut up!"

Chenoa moved toward Chayton on the couch and called the three dogs over to her, rubbing their heads to soothe them. She noticed that Piki must have wandered off.

"So, are there others?" Chayton asked.

"What's with all the questions?" Olivia snipped. "You two talk too much. What about you? Anyone else?"

"No, we haven't seen anyone in almost two years," he said calmly. "Why are you pointing a gun at us? We don't want to hurt you. We're really happy to see other people."

Jack looked at Olivia and rolled his eyes. "How is it that the first people we end up seeing are a bunch of useless brats?" He turned to the children and sneered. "Where are your parents? Did they leave you when all this started because they couldn't stand you?"

Chenoa bristled at the comment, and Chayton's hands rolled into white-knuckled balls. She put her hand on his and squeezed. She understood that these weren't good people. The fact that they carried weapons in the new world said that much about them.

The children listened to the intruders rattle on about their lives over the past two years for over an hour. They had stayed in a hotel up in Munduk in the hills. Everyone had perished, and they'd been living off the gardens and livestock. They had come down to Ubud a month prior and were staying in a hotel across from the villa. They had seen a light on in the villa two nights prior and came across the river the day before to investigate. Since last evening, they'd been spying on the children.

"Let me get you some food and drink. We are happy to see you," Chenoa lied. "Maybe we can look for others together."

"You go get us some food," Olivia spat. "We saw you eatin' meat last night, so cook us up some food. And we aren't your friends, so quit the niceties and all your stupid-ass questions. If you both don't shut up, we're going to shoot one of your dogs and then tape your mouths shut. We don't need our newfound slaves to be talking."

"We aren't going to be your slaves," Chayton shot back, standing.

"Sit DOWN, BOY!" Jack yelled. "And yes, you are our slaves, so get used to it."

"Why don't you go fuck yourself?" Chenoa mumbled as she walked away.

"What's that?" he spewed.

"I said I'll go find a duck for dinner. Don't you like duck?"

"Yeah. Go on then. Cook up a duck, girl. We'll keep the boy here, so don't you think about wandering off."

Chenoa collected a chicken from a flock that wandered around the property, knowing the visitors were too ignorant to tell the difference between chicken and duck. *They obviously can't tell their head from their ass*, she thought.

Afterward, Jack and Olivia sat in the chairs that faced the couch where the kids sat. Jack had tied their feet to prevent them from running. The intruders ate in silence for most of the meal.

"That's a fine duck you cooked, girl," Olivia said as grease and bits of chicken fell down her chin. "Just like we used to eat back in Perth."

"We went to Perth," Chayton said. "Our dad took us to see AC/DC a few years back. They're an amazing Scottish band."

"They're Australian, you little shit!" Jack spewed. "They're from Australia."

"Um, actually Angus and Malcolm were born in Scotland, along with Bon Scott," he said, knowingly taunting his hosts. "So, many people thought they were Scottish."

"Shut up, you stupid American!" Olivia yelled. "You don't know nothing!"

"We're only half American," Chenoa commented, half smirking. "Our mom was born in Canada."

Olivia stood and slapped her across the face. "I'm tired of you two and your nonsense. Little girls like you need to be careful."

Chayton tapped Chenoa's leg. This wasn't the time to antagonize them anymore. And the last thing he wanted was for something to happen to his sister.

"We're sorry," he said. "We're just excited to see people for the first time. But we'll stay quiet."

Jack and Olivia nodded, seeming confident that they had won. The pair kept mumbling about the origins of the AC/DC band members, throwing out expletives toward the children.

Eventually, Jack untied the children's feet and brought them into the living room. He pushed them down with their backs up against the solid teak wood of the interior joglo that commanded the center of the room. He seemed to have some knowledge of knot tying, and the children realized they weren't going to be getting out.

"You'll sleep here tonight with your dogs," Olivia said. "We'll see you in the morning."

The children whispered to each other for the next few hours as the intruders rummaged around the house. They'd heard Jack repeat that they'd hit the jackpot with all the art and valuables here. The children both shook their heads. Their dad used to say that everyone in the world had good in them and that circumstances made people good or bad. But even their dad had limits to this idea. He'd be shaking his head at the absurdity of this situation: it being the end of the world, and two people were still seeking material possessions.

They awoke the next morning to Jack untying their ropes and directing them to make breakfast. The children tried multiple times to engage in discussion but to no avail. The couple had no interest in speaking to them. The children made breakfast for everyone in silence, observing the intruders.

"Hurry up with the damn food, girl," Jack's drippy voice said behind them. "You're a pretty lazy shit." He swatted the back of Chenoa's head, sending her falling forward against the counter.

Chayton charged at Jack, yelling as he slammed into him. His fists hammered into Jack's face as Jack screamed.

"Stop it, or I'll shoot your sister right where she stands," Olivia said.

"You little fucker," Jack spat. He kicked Chayton in the gut and punched his head. "We don't need two of you to cook for us. You want me to choose one of you right now?"

Chayton grabbed his side, but the adrenaline numbed the pain. He glared at the shell of a man. His mom and dad had taught him and Chenoa to be compassionate to others and to understand their stories. But once the family was threatened, it wasn't time for psychological assessments as to what trauma had occurred in their pasts. People needed to assume responsibility at some point.

"Sorry, Jack," Chayton said softly. "I know you'd protect Olivia as well. I was just protecting my sister."

"First, she ain't my sister," Jack spat. "Second, I don't give a shit about her either. She's just a whore I found down in Kuta." He chuckled.

Olivia forced a smile and a laugh.

The next few days were much the same. The children served the intruders and kept to themselves. Jack glared at Chenoa and occasionally smacked Chayton for good measure. Olivia, while slightly more protective of the young girl, participated in the belittling and threats. The dogs kept their distance from the intruders but stayed within protective range of the children.

"How about I cook up a pig tonight?" Chayton asked one day. "We've only been feeding you duck, fish, rice, and vegetables. Maybe we can have a nice meal together. We aren't going to hurt you. Not that we can. You guys are too smart and strong. We're happy to just help you out."

"Well, that'll do," Jack responded. "Glad to see you know your place, boy. Good to see you learning some."

He caught and slaughtered a medium-sized pig that wandered the property and cooked it on the grill. The rich, languid smoke spread through the house and the backyard. The three dogs came near the grill, waiting in line for their food. Chenoa noticed Piki's ears appeared just behind one of the villas, keeping out of sight.

Chayton brought out a fermented, alcoholic ale that he had brought from home.

His sister collected plates and cut big slabs of ribs for Jack and Olivia. She threw the legs to the dogs. "Let's eat on the deck down by the river," she said. "It has a nice view of the valley."

Jack grabbed the bottle of ale from Chayton and sloppily poured glasses for him and Olivia. "Here's to us, Olivia," he said, smiling as he spread out on a weathered lounge chair. "Life's pretty good with these two to take care of us."

He ate his meal and drank most of the ale. But once his speech slurred, he became more belligerent toward the children.

"Boy, you think you're pretty tough, don't you?" he challenged.

"No, I'm just a normal kid, sir," Chayton responded to appease the aggressor.

Chenoa froze in her seat and glanced toward Chayton. They'd managed to keep Jack's attention elsewhere, but they now saw the error in giving this angry man alcohol.

Jack got up and made his way to Chayton. He stood feet apart, hands on his hips. He bent at the waist and put his face directly into Chayton's. The smell of sweat and alcohol hovered about him.

"Leave him alone!" Chenoa ran at Jack to protect her brother, but Jack caught her movement and knocked her to the ground. She flew backward and looked over toward Chayton with fear.

"Leave her alone!" Chayton demanded. He stood to challenge Jack.

Olivia shot a bullet over his head. "You ain't going to do nothing, boy."

The dogs had moved closer already. They inched along on their bellies, toward the children.

Chayton sensed movement behind him. He slightly turned his head and saw that Piki had come up below the deck, just out of sight of Olivia.

"Now, you just shut up," Jack ordered. "I'm done messing around with you both." He stumbled toward Chayton. The dogs stood and snarled at the man, but Olivia fired the gun at them, and they retreated.

Jack stood facing off against the boy. He felt some need to prove his manhood. While life had not deprived him of opportunities, he wanted more. The world owed him.

He raised his hand to Olivia to have her put the gun down. "Come on, boy. You want to fight? Then let's fight."

Chayton didn't hesitate and tackled Jack to the ground. Blows exchanged between the two of them. Chayton cared for nothing except to protect his sister. He was done dealing with this drunken excuse for a man. His capoeira training that he had learned from their Brazilian friend helped him find his balance. He was quicker and stronger than Jack.

He fought with a fury Chenoa had never seen. She witnessed her brother become a man at that moment. She felt protected and loved as she feared for his life.

Chayton struck Jack with a blow that knocked him to the ground. As he moved toward Jack, he didn't notice him reaching down to his boot to pull out a knife. The knife whipped across the air, just missing his chest. Jack stumbled to his feet and put the knife in Chayton's face.

"You're going to pay for that, boy." He raised the knife above his head to strike Chayton.

A large thump sounded behind Jack on the wooden decking.

Jack turned to face a towering striped beast whose eyes pierced into his. "What the fu—"

A paw struck his face. Olivia screamed and raised her gun to fire. But Piki darted past Chenoa and locked his jaws onto Olivia's arm, ripping her flesh. The gun fired, hitting Jack's shoulder.

"What are you doing, woman?!" he yelled as he grabbed at the bleeding wound.

Piki snapped her arm, and the gun fell onto the deck. Jack reached for it, but the tiger swiped down on his arm. He backed away with his hands held in front of him.

The tiger jumped down from the bench and stalked toward Jack. He screamed to Olivia for help, but she sat motionless and in shock, surrounded by the dogs. Tigger lunged, knocking Jack to the floor. She lumbered atop the man, her face inches from his. And then it was over.

"You need to leave now!" Chenoa commanded Olivia.

The woman scrambled away and crossed the footbridge to the other side of the river. She would not be returning, knowing the children were protected by tigers and a pack of dogs.

Chenoa and Chayton moved away from the tiger and Jack's lifeless body. They were relieved that their captors were gone and thankful for Tigger and the dogs. But they were in shock by what they had just witnessed.

He put his arm around her and hugged her. She turned into him and cried. He held her for a long time, happy that the ordeal was over.

"Thank you, Chayton. Thank you for standing up to them."

"Thank god for Tigger and the dogs," he whispered.

The siblings packed their belongings in silence and headed home.

A coucal called from a tree.

CHAPTER 16

THE BAMBOO SCHOOL

THE CHILDREN HUDDLED inside their villa for the next few days, only venturing out together and with the dogs to collect food. They filled the generator with diesel, kept the gates and doors locked, and turned on the lights within the villa. The dogs patrolled the grounds and slept outside. Nothing could now enter without them sounding the alarm.

The children debated leaving the lights off at night since perhaps the light became a beacon to others. The lights ended up staying on, but they still sensed someone watching them from across the valley. They knew it was irrational, just as monsters under their beds weren't possible. But they still checked under their beds.

As they sought safety, they also desired comfort in familiar things. Chenoa wanted popcorn, and as soon as she mentioned it to her brother, he had it on his mind. They took the truck, but the engine's roar unsettled them as the noise cut through the silence. They wanted to remain inconspicuous, hidden from other watchers.

Their trips were always quick and efficient now. One would watch the door as the other shopped for supplies. As they rushed back to the truck, they'd slam the locks shut.

They drizzled coconut oil and salt on the popcorn and decided on *Love Actually*, a family favorite that they'd watch most years around Christmas. The movie ended after the children had fallen asleep on the couch.

"What if there are others, Chay?" Chenoa asked one day while they lounged in their living room.

"That is a possibility. But now we need to consider that even if we do find others, they aren't going to be nice. I got Olivia's gun, and they had a bunch of bullets in their backpack. Jack also had a gun. We can practice out back later."

"I'm never letting that happen to me again. Thanks for protecting me."

"You stood up for me as well. And you had some pretty funny *duck* comments. What a bunch of fools." He laughed.

But she didn't laugh. Her nights were restless, and every shadow—to her—was an intruder. She was comforted Jack was gone and that Olivia was no longer a threat to them.

Chayton put his arm around her and guided her to the kitchen for lunch.

She sat at the table, still looking pale. "They were evil, Chay. How can people be that twisted?"

"I don't know. Nature or nurture? Were they born that way, or did society make them like that?"

"Dad felt that it was partially because schools screwed people up," she added. "He talked about it all the time. What did he call it? Spiritual disconnect, I think. Both he and Mom hated the idea that schools mostly focused on grades and tests and getting into a university and then getting a job when people were ultimately unhappy with their work."

"Parents and teachers discussed it all the time when they'd come from other schools," Chayton added. "Kids really hated school. I remember Dad had a bunch of statistics about how bored and depressed kids were around the world."

"Not just bored," she said. "Kids were also killing themselves. Remember all those kids killing themselves at the high school near Stanford University? They had to put people at the train crossings to make sure kids didn't jump in front of the trains."

"That is just so messed up. What was society thinking? Kids are depressed and hurting themselves, but no one wants to change the system?"

"It was a big reason Mom and Dad wanted us to come to Green School," she added. "But even Green School had its issues."

"Ya think?!" He laughed. "Want to go check it out? I bet it's a damn jungle there now with no one maintaining it. Let's go."

They packed the truck with all four dogs, provisions, baseball bats, and machetes. Chayton grabbed both guns and hid them under his seat without telling Chenoa. He knew she wouldn't disagree with bringing them, but he didn't want to add to her anxiety.

The truck turned onto the main road, and the deep blue sky brightened their moods. She rolled down her window, and he followed. As the sun and warm air fluttered on her face, she closed her eyes. Machi pushed her face next to hers.

They passed the school's entrance. Chenoa caught sight of the bamboo school sign along the ground, noting its red and white coloring. The school's colors were green and white, but the government mandated bureaucracy had insisted that schools create signs to align with the national colors. Red and white signs had sprung up all over the island.

Chayton forced the truck through the half-hidden entrance, and limbs clawed at the truck's sides. She covered her ears as a piercing nails-down-a-chalkboard sound ripped through the cab. She shook and put her head between her knees, triggered by the violent noise.

"I'm sorry, Chenoa." Her brother put his hand on her shaking back. "There isn't much room for the truck." He shook his head as he looked at his terrified sister. *Four people left in the world and half of them caused trauma. I'm glad Tigger ate those bastards.*

The guard house had fallen over and lay strewn to one side in a pile of pickup sticks. The Kembali Recycling Centre had suffered a similar fate. They passed Warung Ajik and Soogi Roll. Their dad ate at Soogi Roll every day. Sometimes twice.

Chayton stopped the truck in front of the school's main entrance. He started to open his door, but Chenoa put her hand on his arm.

"Just a second, Chay."

She rolled down her window and listened. Chirping insects and Machi's panting were the only noises that came to her ears. The other dogs were quiet in the truck bed.

She then opened her door, and he followed. The dogs leaped out and stayed close. The children leaned onto the handle to slide open the main gate. The rusted door moaned, alerting the area to their presence.

The campus' river stone driveway had disappeared into the newly formed jungle.

Green School was a progressive, environmentally oriented school. It had been started by Cynthia and John Hardy, a couple who had made their money in the jewelry business and wanted a different experience for their children. Most buildings were made of intricately designed bamboo structures, some multiple stories. The campus boasted no air conditioners, except for one required by the bank to keep their ATM cool. This irony was not lost on the parents as the money was kept cool and clean, but the children were sweaty and muddy.

Chayton went to the school for ten years and graduated. He had jumped from a traditional school in Singapore to a bamboo one in Bali. He knew it was different the first day he had arrived. Teachers and parents openly talked about the "ambitious project."

He had loved the school and had been less aware of the challenges of running a school when his dad was the Director. But somehow the teachers, staff, and families who were attracted to the school created a phenomenal community, challenges and all.

In some ways, Green School was a microcosm of the world with governance challenges, uprisings, and rebirths. It happened often enough that one might wonder if it was a necessary part of life.

He chuckled to himself as he looked at the jungle in front of him. "This was a pretty special place, wasn't it, Chenoa?"

"Yeah, I sure miss it. There were a lot of really great people here, and some very cool things happened on campus. In the end, the focus on the students always brought things back down to earth."

"Remember when Mom said we were condo children when we first arrived, and within a few months we'd become feral?" he smirked. He wavered as he looked at all the greenery around them. "Let's go inside."

"Hey Chay, we are the only alumni left from the school."

"We might be the only *people* left in the world," he corrected.

"Where is the school anyway? I can barely see the paths."

"Are you sure you want to go in there?"

"No. Yes. I'm not sure. Let's go," she said. "I want to see what it looks like. And I brought a basketball for the gym."

Chayton led the way and turned off to the right to enter a decrepit building. "It's The Bridge, Chenoa. What Dad, Carol, and Kate started."

She moved into the bamboo structure. Trees and vines covered the outside, so little light made its way in. She remembered her dad talking to parents and visitors, listening to their stories, and helping them follow their interests. He had loved the team, particularly Ugie who helped start The Bridge. He would talk about the wonderful stories she wrote for her son. He also would bring the team ice cream on Wednesdays as a small thank you.

An eeriness echoed through the empty, open-walled bamboo structure. The recycled denim couch in the back had been overrun with rats, and a dog slept on one of the chairs. The large mural of a bridge made of plastic and sandals collected from the beach hung askew on the back wall. They wiped off a table and pushed the vines that weaved across the floor aside. They then sat, sipping their water and nibbling on a fruit snack. The dogs explored the abandoned building and surrounding area but did not wander off too far.

"Can't you kind of feel all of them, Chay?" Chenoa asked after a moment. "If I close my eyes, I can hear Carol speaking in Portuguese and Ugie helping a parent. And how often did we come here to see Dad sitting on that couch and talking to a student or a parent or meeting with the Writer's Club?"

"And how often would he keep talking when we wanted to go?" He laughed. "But I'd take that back now. I'd give anything to have them all back. Let's go, Chenoa."

They hacked with their machetes to clear a path along the pond. A deer drank from the water. Ducks waddled along the edge but swam away as the children passed.

The grand Sangkep assembly hall opened to their left. A young visitor had once said that the building reminded her of a dragon since the bamboo intertwined to create a long, intricate structure. The siblings winced as the smell of ammonia hit them. They looked up to see a vibrating ceiling covered with bats. They walked to the center and stood still. A part of the ceiling had collapsed as a tree pushed over a supporting bamboo pole. Chenoa remembered seeing Dr. Jane Goodall, Vandana Shiva, Sylvia Earle, and many other important people come to this building to talk to the kids. Children had sung and danced on the stage. Elaborate musicals and shows had been held to packed halls of five hundred sweaty people. They had even danced to Michael Franti when he had visited.

But now the building was a shadow of its former self. Music and laughter would never grace its halls again.

"It's depressing, isn't it?" Chay whispered to Chenoa.

"Totally. But we always knew it would end up like this."

"What do you mean?"

"Even without the volcanoes wiping things out, all of this would have been gone someday anyway. Maybe not for another hundred years or so, but it would be gone. Dad explained this to me once. He had found it weird that people spent so much time holding onto things when it all went away eventually. He liked to talk about life in a thousand or hundred thousand years. Some people thought it was foolish. But he was right. Time doesn't stop. And a billion years will come at some point."

"Mom felt the same," he added. "They both seemed to understand how temporal life was."

"Ooh, *temporal*. Where did you learn that word?" she teased him.

"Shut up. Let's go."

The gym's undulating, wavey rooftop sat across the soccer field. The field was overgrown with waist-high grass. The dogs disappeared into the grass, but Chayton called them back, concerned about snakes and other animals. They moved together as a pack. Chenoa led the way, stomping her feet to warn the snakes along their path ahead.

The gym had suffered the same fate as the Sangkep, except there were no bats. Perhaps they liked to congregate in the other building. Pumpkin vines wove across the floor. One vine had traveled from one side to the other, seeking sunlight. Five large orange pumpkins grew from its ends. The children dragged the vines to the edges. Gecko and bird poop covered the floor, but this was nothing new for the children who had grown accustomed to animals crapping on their chairs and tables at school each night.

"Hey, Chay! Catch!" Chenoa yelled as she threw the basketball to him.

The loud echo of the bouncing ball made him freeze. He felt as if she had just signaled their location to the world. His sister seemed to have a similar reaction.

"You okay?" he asked.

"Just so loud. These used to be such normal sounds. Now they bother me."

He just nodded. She hadn't been the same since the intruders. And rightly so.

He dribbled and shot an airball.

Chenoa ran to the ball, laughing as it rolled to the back netting. "Ha! Nice shot, dumbass."

"Okay. You try it. I haven't played in years," he defended. "Let's see what you can do."

She dribbled back and forth and took a mid-range shot. The net whipped upward as the ball sailed through the rim. She shuffled her feet in celebration and heckled her brother.

They played H-O-R-S-E for the next hour. Chayton had size and height, but she had quickness and speed. Most importantly, they lost any interest in winning, just celebrating their time together.

They laughed and chased each other. They remembered their mom and dad playing in the gym with the teachers and staff. Their dad had loved to play inside where all the pushing and shoving happened. His dribbling had been questionable. Their mom had played in college and was a smarter player with a better outside shot.

The children eventually collected their things and called to the dogs as they made their way to the center of Green School, also called the Heart of School.

"Chayton, let's go see if my fairy house is still there," Chenoa said.

They walked past the bright white Luke Skywalker building, one of the few non-bamboo structures on campus. It had been a class project to build out of recycled materials and became the media lab and marketing center. It had been beautifully designed but stuck out like a sore thumb. They passed the solar panels and wound their way to her classroom.

The fairy house still stood albeit covered in growth. Her class had done a lesson on useful fairies. One of the children had asked if they could build a fairy house. In a normal school, the suggestion would have been dismissed. But Chenoa's teacher had nodded and sought out Elora, the head of design for the bamboo buildings. She had sat with the children, got all their inputs, and designed the two-meter high, double story bamboo structure. She even built it with the children. This was the magic of Green School.

"I can't believe it's still here, Chay." She ran her hand across it. "Let's look inside."

They pushed their way through the underbrush and peeked inside the diminutive structure. Huddled inside was a baby deer.

"It is so cute, Chay!" She smiled. "I wonder where its mom is. I can't believe there is a baby deer in the house. What a perfect home."

"Yeah, well, where there are deer, there are probably animals that eat the deer. Let's leave it here."

They entered the Heart of School, which was said to be the largest bamboo structure in the world. The school was known for its marketing hyperbole. The structure consisted of three separate multi-story bamboo buildings that were interconnected with walkways. From an aerial view, the rooftops formed three swirling structures made out of alangalang, a Balinese grass.

The building had been the centerpiece of Green School. It was the venue for daily lunches, musicals, and student-led events. Visitors and guests could pay to have their names engraved on the bamboo poles by the local carver. Their dad had Chayton's and Chenoa's names engraved on the poles near Dr. Jane Goodall's name. Now, thousands of carvings decorated the poles, like names on tombstones in a lost cemetery.

They walked down to the bridge. The original bridge had been washed away. The new Millennium Bridge was named in celebration of the millennium goals to ensure the sustainability of the world.

"Everything's gone, Chenoa," Chay noted as he looked at the plants overgrowing along the bridge. "All those years of work and building, and the world just eats it up in two years. Green School is gone. Bali is gone. The world is gone. Everything."

"I'm not sure nature is eating things up or tearing them down. Nature is *definitely* reclaiming her role. I think she has been fighting back for a long time. We were like cockroaches. There were eight billion of us roaming around and screwing things up. Maybe the volcanoes weren't an accident."

"That's silly. Of course it was just some natural event."

"Maybe. But some people used to think that Earth was a singular living organism, a microbiome. Plants and trees and animals and fungi all spoke with each other. Maybe they said they'd had enough of our shit and decided to blow the whole thing up."

"No way," he responded. "Well, maybe."

Chenoa pointed down to the river. "Look, Chay!"

A herd of elephants played in the water. The school was downstream on the same river as their home, so they weren't sure if it was the same herd they had seen before or another one. But they smiled at the sight of elephants playing in the river, nevertheless.

They then turned back to gaze upon a place that had been a part of their lives for over a decade. Memories of teachers, friends, and parents ran through their minds. A once well-known place where thousands of people would visit each year was simply another lost relic.

They turned their backs and left the Green School one last time.

CHAPTER 17

THE DEEP

STORM DEBRIS LITTERED the coastal road to Padangbai, slowing the siblings' progress on the normally well-managed four-lane road. The truck made the passage easier with its four-wheel drive, but they wondered when the roads would eventually become impassable to motorized vehicles. At the same time, the lack of dangerous, speeding drivers made the trip feel like a Sunday drive in rural Oklahoma.

The dogs had remained behind to safeguard the house. Chenoa had insisted that they lock the doors and gates, and Chayton did not question it. As he drove, he subconsciously felt for the gun bag behind his seat. She caught his movement and forced a smile. While months had passed since the intruders had abducted them, she still slept restlessly, often waking from nightmarish sweats. She slept in the same room as Chayton and the dogs now, but he had never questioned nor teased her about it.

Hearty seaside plants had sprung up along the typically overly manicured roadsides. The trees leaned into the coastal winds, pushing back against the tropical weather. They also pushed through the paved parking lots, which were stopping points for tourists to snack in the warungs and to buy trinkets from young girls carrying display trays. Only posts remained from the bamboo bales and shops that had dotted the beachside lots. Newly formed mangroves filled pockets along the coast, protecting the land from erosion. No boats moored in the shallow bay and covers. Frigates, terns, and brown boobys glided about the skies, playing in the coastal updrafts and searching for midday snacks along the shoreline.

Padangbai was a small port town. Ferries had transported people and cars out to the neighboring Gili Islands and Lombok. The siblings now drove through the desolate center of town and saw a similar fate as the other towns: empty, degraded, and crumbling.

An empty harbor awaited them at the end of the main road. Hundreds of boats typically adorned the bay. Now, the only remaining boats clung to the main dock. All the others had been pulled from their anchor lines and moorings. The one-hundred-car ferry was missing, either still at port on another island or dislodged and floating aimlessly at sea.

They pulled in front of OK *Divers*, a Czech-owned and family-run diving center and hotel where they had done all their open water and advanced open water PADI training with their dad. The hotel now sat empty, a lifeless shell. A twinge of sadness came over them as they recollected the times they had there.

They gathered their things and headed inside. The entrance opened to an algae-green deep pool and restaurant.

"Wouldn't you love one of their fried Czech potato pancakes with that garlicky yogurt sauce right now?" Chenoa asked. "Oh my god. I'm so hungry."

Chayton ignored her.

They walked through to the hotel and another mossy green pool before making their way to the third floor. The hotel was a small boutique, painted white with a European feel. The doors had electric locks, but the windows had been cracked open. The rooms were not mold ridden and fairly clean outside of a bit of gecko poop and spiders. They found the larger three-bedroom family room that they had stayed in before, climbed in through the windows, and dropped their bags.

As soon as they did, Chayton got up to head downstairs.

"Where you going, Chay?" his sister asked.

"To see what the diving equipment looks like," he responded as he picked up a bag.

"That's not a good idea. You didn't say we'd go diving. We don't know how to fill the tanks, and there is no electricity anyway. You aren't thinking as usual."

"Why would we come all the way out here and not dive?" he snapped back.

"Chayton..."

"Che. No. A!" he blurted. "I want to go diving. If you don't want to come, then fine by me." He didn't want to go by himself, but he knew she wouldn't let him go alone.

She didn't appreciate his game. "You're a jerk."

He went on ahead, pushed open the door to the equipment room, and was hit by a strong waft of mildew. He grabbed fins, weights, a mask, and a BCD and laid them out in the sun next to his dad's wetsuit that he had taken out of the bag. He was proud he fit into his dad's suit now. He returned to find a suit that looked about Chenoa's size.

He found the air filling station in the back. A few tanks were partially full, but he wanted to refill them since the air would have gone bad. He discovered a generator in the back room, and after he pulled the cord for about twenty minutes, the engine roared to life. Laminated instructions for filling the tanks were tacked to the back wall. He fully emptied a tank, which he felt was a good sign that it still held pressure, attached the nozzle, and filled it to the two hundred bar. He filled another for Chenoa and brought them out to the equipment outside. He attached the BCD, sniffed the air, and decided that it smelled fine. He then proceeded to take a few breaths to check the quality. His teen-scientific-research approach gave him enough confidence that everything was fine.

"Chenoa, try your air," he said. "It seems good to me. The equipment looks okay, and the suits are still in good shape. Come on." He knew the eventual outcome would be her coming along, but he wanted her to come along willingly. "We can drive over to Blue Lagoon and go from the shore instead of from a boat. If it isn't working then, we are right at the shore." He chuckled. "What can go wrong?"

"You are a fool," she said with her arms crossed. "If Radka and Dan were around, they'd revoke your certificate."

"Well, they aren't, and as far as I can tell, there isn't a PADI anymore, so you and I can set the rules. I've just personally upgraded my credentials to a master diver instructor. Let's go."

Chenoa succumbed and collected her equipment. They loaded up the truck and drove just north over the ridge from Padangbai to Blue Lagoon.

As they pulled into the parking lot, vast azure water unfolded in front of them. The bay had been previously mottled with boats, fishermen, and trash. Yet now here stood a Louvre-worthy painting composed of a simple palette of blue, white, and green for the ocean, beach, and trees. They dressed in their wetsuits and brought the equipment to the blindingly bright white beach.

"It is so beautiful," Chayton said. "It's amazing."

"You sound like Dad. He thought everything was amazing."

"Well, this is amazing. It doesn't even look the same. Do you even see one piece of garbage? All the boats are gone. And smell the air. It smells *alive*."

"Okay, Homer. Not sure about that. But this is wild. Look over there." She pointed. "Have you ever seen so many seabirds? And turtles!"

The bay was alive with life. Gulls dived into the surf, reappearing with silver treasure in their beaks. A small flock of boobys searched the water's edge for crabs and other crustaceans. The tide ebbed and flowed as if the ocean was breathing. The bay was infinitely busier with marine and animal life but also calming at the same time.

The siblings donned their equipment, walked through their checks, and planned their dive. They'd kick out to conserve air and then dive about fifty meters from the shore. Since they had already dived into the bay many times, they were familiar with the terrain. The bay was protected, and the diving was mostly within a ten-to-twenty-meter depth, so no fear of decompression sickness. They plodded through the moderate surf and kicked on their backs to their dive entry.

Chayton and Chenoa gave each other the okay sign and submerged.

The children dropped to the ocean floor and rested on the sandy bottom. The view could only be explained as an animated Monet. Their mouths dropped in front of an Impressionist landscape.

Millions of creatures swarmed the waters. Hundreds of blacktip sharks circled above, appearing only as silhouettes against the sun's rays. A swirling school of tuna spanned fifty meters and reflected the light. Teethy barracudas patrolled the area. The children pointed and spun in a 360 degree turn, pulling at each other's arms to show off other animals that appeared in their window.

Chayton tapped his sister and pointed. An enormous brownish-red octopus crawled along the ocean floor, just meters in front of them. Its legs spanned over two meters in diameter as it searched nooks and crannies for food. Octopuses were usually nocturnal, but this creature was midday lunching. It paused as it noticed the new arrivals.

It then strolled toward the children, extended its tentacles, and fingered their masks. Their eyes widened, and they reached for each other to share their excitement. The tentacles reached around them and connected on their backsides. They panicked for a moment, believing they were going to be squeezed, but the creature only gently hugged them in what seemed like some peculiar greeting. Chenoa extended her hand and brushed the octopus' head. It retracted its tentacles and floated away.

They stayed in the same spot for over thirty minutes, too awestruck to move. In their excitement, they lost the practiced, steady control of their breathing. They didn't notice their oxygen levels dropping on their gauges.

They moved along the sandy ocean floor and toward the coral beds in the south. Newly formed coral populated the ocean floor and led a path to a rocky coral wall, which erupted with a rainbow of colors. Nudibranchs, the radiantly colored soft-bodied gastropods, adorned the walls. The elegant creatures were typically difficult to find given their size, shyness, and population decline, but now the walls danced with the gentle beings. Clownfish played in the sea anemones. Reticent eels protruded from the crevices.

Stonefish. Scorpionfish. Pufferfish. Cuttlefish. Lobsters. The *Nemo* animators would have been impressed.

The children explored and poked about in the new world. They were like two kids in a candy shop. They pointed, waved, darted, and dived.

A dark shadow passed over the divers, blocking the sun. Chayton looked up to see a ten-meter whale shark with a calf swimming overhead. He reached to tap his sister but ended up tapping empty space. He turned to her, but she was gone.

Safety training flashed in his mind. He looked at his pressure gauge: fifty bars. They should have been ascending already. He spun in a circle, but there was no sign of her. He knew the PADI rules were to search for one minute and then surface, but something told him otherwise. He slowed his breath to preserve his air. She usually lasted longer on the dives since she managed her breathing better and utilized less air, but now...

He cursed himself for being so flippant with their safety. He then focused, knowing his emotions wouldn't help. Their mom's voice rang in his ears. *Always protect each other.*

He turned to swim away when a yellow flash caught his attention. It was a lone butterfly fish. He followed the fish with his eyes, curious as to why the typically shy fish was away from its protective home.

Behind the yellow fish, a coral pinnacle rose from the ocean floor a few meters in front of him. *How have I not seen it before?* He kicked over and came around to the other side. Fins protruded from an outcrop at the rock's base. He dived to find Chenoa, oblivious to the fact that she had lost her diving buddy. Relieved and angry, he tapped her arm.

She tried to turn, and he saw her wide eyes. He signed to ask if she was okay. She responded with a flat hand, rotating up and down. She had a problem. He reached for her air indicator and noticed that she was down to five bars.

He pointed for her to go up, but she flared about. He then grabbed her legs, but she wouldn't move. She was locked in place. He knew not to panic, but he was fighting fear. He looked around her tank and saw that its valve had wedged itself between two rock plates. He pushed her forward, dislodged her, and pulled her out.

But she was out of air.

He reached for his buddy air regulator and handed it to her. She placed it into her mouth and inhaled. Relief set in her eyes. Along with tears.

They surfaced to five meters and made a three-minute safety stop. He noticed that he had ten bars left in his tank, so they continued their ascent. They surfaced and inflated their BCDs.

He immediately turned to his sister. "Chenoa, are you okay?"

"I..." She burst into tears. "I'm so sorry, Chay. I'm so, so sorry. I was so scared when I got trapped. I knew you weren't coming because you were supposed to surface." She sobbed and sucked for air. "How did you know? Why did you come?"

"I don't know. I just knew something wasn't right." He reached for her awkwardly and tried to give her a hug. He started to explain the yellow butterfly fish that turned his attention to where she had been trapped but decided against it. *There is no way*, he thought.

She wrapped her arms around his neck, and they stayed that way for a few minutes, bobbing in the surf.

"I'm so sorry I made you do this," he said. "It is my fault. I was a fool."

"No, no. It was beautiful, Chay. Just beautiful. I'm so glad we did it, and I'm just so glad you found me. I'm okay. I'm really okay."

They floated together in the quiet bay. The terror and tears subsided to the gentle, rocking waves. Eventually, they kicked back to shore on their backs side by side, holding onto each other's arms. Tears occasionally reappeared in the siblings' eyes.

Chay held her arm a little bit tighter than usual.

CHAPTER 18

BUTTERFLY

THE CHILDREN DROVE home after the dive, wanting to get back to the dogs and to the comfort of their home. They barely spoke on the trip back. As they pulled into the garage, the dogs clamored to the gate. Machi pushed her face through the fence's gap. Chenoa slid the gate open and sat in the middle of the eager dogs as they licked her face and nuzzled her for love. She giggled and hugged them.

Chayton sat for a bit and patted Kuma. "You okay, Chenoa?"

"I think so."

He saw tears strolling down her face. He was happy to see her surrounded by the dogs she loved so much. He knew their mom was sitting nearby as well, smiling at her. *Is this her life now? Is she left with just me and the animals around her?*

Kubi jumped into her lap, and she rolled back laughing.

Chayton put his head between his knees and held back tears. *How can I ever offer her enough in life?*

He walked into the house and sat on the couch in the center of the living room, facing the valley. The four six-meter teak posts of the joglo framed the room's center. Their mom had told them that she and their dad had sat in this exact spot when they had leased the land. Their contractor had built a bamboo seating area at the same height as where their future seating would be to offer them a perspective on what it would be like in their home. Chayton closed his eyes and imagined his parents sitting on the bench with nothing else around as they looked out over the green valley. *What were they thinking as they sat looking at the same view?*

He was tired, empty. The episode with the river, the intruders, and Chenoa's diving experience had taken a toll on him. *I can't do this anymore*, he thought. *I just can't do it, Mom and Dad.*

A fluttering motion out near the pool caught his attention. At first, he thought it was small birds playing. But he stepped out onto the porch to a kaleidoscope of butterflies. Thousands—if not hundreds of thousands—of colorful dancing faeries flitted over the pool and about the yard. They swarmed the hill and the embankment down toward the river. The butterflies were larger than any he'd ever seen with brilliant deep blues, emerald greens, vivid reds, and multicolored. The scene was too surreal.

"Chenoa!" he called. "Chenoa!"

"What?! Why are you yelling? Oh my..." She stepped next to him. "What is happening, Chay?"

The children sat on the deck stairs, watching nature's version of *The Nutcracker*. The dogs came and sat beside them. The pups tilted their heads from side to side as they observed the dancing imagery. Kubi lunged forward to chase and play with the new toys. He jumped up and down, struggling to grab at the gentle kites.

A purple butterfly, about the size of his hand, gently landed on Chayton's arm. Its wings opened and closed in a slow rhythmic motion. He moved his hand toward the butterfly, and it crawled up onto his fingers. He turned his hand back and forth to examine the magnificent creature.

"Chay, do you remember the story about the butterfly from Dad?" Chenoa asked.

"He had mentioned it. I don't remember all of it though."

"His younger brother had called to tell him that John had been diagnosed with terminal brain cancer," Chenoa explained in a somber voice. "John's third child was due in a couple of months. Mom and Dad were living in Japan then. Dad immediately packed up and left for California to be with them."

"And I had just been born, right?" Chayton asked. "I think Mom put me on a plane at four months and went to be with Dad."

"Yeah. That's right. But the wild thing was that John was a doctor, and his wife was a nurse. So, the moment they got the news, they knew it was a death sentence. They told him he had nine months to live."

"Mom said that Dad went into a pretty dark place," he added. "He and his brothers were sometimes called The

Three Bears. Grandma always had pictures of bears up around the house."

"It's strange since we talk about death quite a bit as a family. Mom's mom died, and Dad's dad and brother died. I don't think many families like to talk about death."

"No one *likes* to talk about death, Chenoa. But people in Asia definitely talk about it more openly. People don't seem afraid of it here. Americans don't ever talk about it, like it's not going to happen. Dad's mom even used to say that she had friends who would say, '*If* I die, then...' They couldn't even say *when*."

"Dad had said that John had the most incredible mind. He...he hated seeing him die like that." Chenoa paused and composed herself. "Do you remember when he died?"

"Of course. He died on the eighteenth of December, the day before my birthday. That time of year is so weird. Death, birth, and then Christmas. I sometimes wish I had been born in June."

"I know. I felt bad for you. Mom and Dad always struggled with it as well. I think that is why they threw you that off-cycle birthday party. Remember that?"

"Oh god, yes. That was Dad. Pink flamingo blow-up floaties in the pool, cake, and all the normal birthday stuff. I know he was just having some fun, but damn that was gaudy."

"Gaaawwwdeeeee!" Chenoa repeated in an English accent.

He ignored her and moved on. "I was there when Uncle John died. There is a photo of me sitting on his chest just a few days before. Everyone was around him when he died. Dad sat next to him and drank a Coors Light. He kept that bottle somewhere. And he took his St. Christopher's necklace and placed it on John's head for a moment. That was so sad. They'd traveled all over the world to Africa and to the Amazon, but then it all got taken away."

"What if you die, Chay?"

He measured his response, given everything that had happened. "What do you mean? I'm not going to die."

"You almost did. And then I almost did. One of us is going to be left alone someday."

He shifted and fumbled with his fingers. He didn't like discussing death even though it was about the only thing that was constant these past two years. He wanted to move on from the conversation but then reconsidered. "One of us will die someday, Chenoa. There is nothing we can do about that. We can't bring back Mom and Dad or any of our friends. But we don't totally go away."

"What do you mean?"

"I think you are forgetting the last part of that story. Dad was lying in their bedroom in Tokyo and looking out into a small Japanese garden. He was happy because it was raining. He liked that kind of weather. Made him feel safe. Anyway, he is looking out the window, and a butterfly flutters into the garden. He had never seen a butterfly in their garden before. It came to rest on a fern, waving its wings back and forth."

"He thought it was John, didn't he?" Chenoa cut in.

"Yep. He was convinced it was John. Then when he looked into it, he found out that butterflies can often be spirits coming back into our world."

"That's why there is that butterfly pin under his computer. And did you ever notice that metal butterfly in the yard outside his office?"

"What butterfly?" Chayton looked confused. "There isn't anything there."

He looked over and realized that he had forgotten about the butterfly resting on his hand. He carefully stood to not send it flying away. It continued to rest on his hand. The siblings walked around the corner of the deck, and she pointed to a weathered, metal butterfly that sat attached to a metal rod.

"He brought it from his mom's house," she told him. "She had it in her yard, and he took it when they sold the house."

"I can't believe it. That has been sitting here for almost two years, and I've never noticed that." He shook his head and brushed the metal butterfly with his free hand.

"Do you think that is Dad or Mom on your hand?"

"I'm not sure. I hope not because then..."

"Yes, I know. But maybe he and Mom just sent them to check in on us."

"I think they may have overdone it," he said, pointing to the thousands of butterflies fluttering in the breeze.

Chenoa laughed and smiled at her brother. "I don't know what has happened in the world, and I have no idea what will happen tomorrow, Chay. But I'm glad we have each other at least. Maybe there is some lesson or meaning in all this shit. I have no idea. But I can say that seeing nature come back and all these butterflies around us must mean something. Don't you think?"

"I do. I can't explain it either, but there is a buzz in the world, if that makes sense. It used to feel like my energy was leaving, but now it feels like the world gives me energy. I don't know. That sounds weird."

"Not at all. I feel the same way. It's like electricity is flowing through everything, a resonance. I swear I can feel the world vibrating."

He smiled. "Me too, sis. Me too."

The siblings started up a fire and grilled some fish and vegetables. Chenoa opened a coconut and mixed it with some passion fruit. They sat quietly as the sun sank behind them to the west.

The world breathed. Inhaling, exhaling. It was at peace.

The few remaining butterflies fluttered away.

Chayton put his arm around his sister, and she leaned into him. "It'll be okay, Chenoa."

She hugged him back.

A white butterfly flew behind the children and rested on the wooden towel rack next to the purple butterfly. Their wings moved in rhythm as they watched over the children.

CHAPTER 19

TREE

"TURN HERE," CHENOA directed, pointing toward a dirt road.

"Why?" her brother asked.

"Just turn here, Chayton. I want to see something."

He reluctantly turned the truck down the dirt road off the main bypass through Sanur. They were heading south to explore Jimbaran, the small bulbous part of Bali that sat south of the airport. Their daily outings were routine to gather supplies and find signs of human life. Except for the intruders, they had found no other people. But they continued to look, nevertheless. Because once they decided to stop looking, any hope for their parents would be gone.

Perhaps it was a charade as they realized the futility. But hope was a powerful motivator.

"What are we doing?" he asked. "This is that stinky garbage dump road. I came here years ago. It's a shithole. And those fires that burned toxic smoke across Bali? We could see them from the airplane. This is silly, Chenoa."

"Just go a bit further. Please, Chay."

The road wound toward the coast and the Suwung garbage dump. He had been there years ago on a school trip. It had depressed him for weeks. He didn't understand how the government allowed the dump to leak into the waterways and destroy the surrounding land. It had been home to a few hundred families who lived nearby and extracted a meager income from recycling items.

"Look, Chay! Look!"

The mountains of plastic were no longer visible. A thick verdant blanket covered the hills, and trees and plants grew in spotty patches. Birds covered the landscape, pecking about the hillside. A cow chewed its food, its gaze following the truck as it passed. A family of black pigs rooted around a tight outcropping of shrubs. Deer grazed along the slopes.

The children got out of the truck and walked toward the lush hills. The contrast between what they had seen before and now was mind-boggling. The smoky, steamy piles of putrid garbage that extended for over a kilometer had turned into an image similar to the rolling hills of New Zealand.

Mother Nature had healed a festering wound.

They approached the edge of the hills. Chayton cautiously stepped forward, testing the ground. It was firm with a spongy give. He grabbed a stick and dug into the earth. A dense mesh of plants and roots provided a thick blanket of cover. As he dug deeper, he came to a thriving, bustling microbial world. He found a glass bottle, but there was no sign of any plastic. Something had consumed all the plastic, and life had returned to the hills that had been devoid of it.

A black pig wandered nearby, digging for food and insects. It ignored the children and tunneled about the base of a tree.

"Does he make you hungry, Chenoa?" Chayton teased his sister. "Should I tell him to run?"

"Funny," she snapped. "Why don't you go root around with him and find some grubs, pighead."

"What was that book Dad always talked about? You know, the one about the world that lived underground and connected all the trees and plants?" he asked, changing the topic.

"*The Overstory*. The book was called *The Overstory*. He said it was one of his favorites."

They both chuckled since their dad had *many* favorites.

"He said it was *amazing*," she added.

"I think the book was right," he admitted. "Look at this. Imagine what is happening in the rest of the world."

He understood the world beneath their feet. He had taken soil assessment courses and studied the microbial world for his work with Junglo. He understood the microbiome *well*. It was not composed of separate parts.

"Like the Ents in *Lord of the Rings*," he continued. "They communicated with each other. The water systems are connected, and the root structures are interconnected. Nature is a singular symbiotic being. There was always this hidden, flourishing world that consumed invaders. The only thing that threw the world off balance was humankind."

"That was pretty impressive," Chenoa complimented. "You sounded like a teacher!"

They trudged up the hill, carefully stepping since they didn't want to fall through the top layer. But the hill held. An African tulip tree sat atop the hill, displaying its bright reddish-orange flowers. It stood five meters high, and its canopy spread to give the children a reprieve from the midday heat. They leaned against its trunk and gazed out toward the ocean. Green hills contrasted against the vast blue waters.

"This is what Bali is supposed to look like, Chenoa," Chayton muttered.

A pod of whales moved southward, sending up spouts of water. The leader breached and crashed back into the water. The giant spray created a momentary rainbow. Its tail slapped against the surface, sending an audible crack toward the watchers on the hill.

She brought out their dried mango and water from her backpack. "It's genesis, Chay."

"It's what?! *Genesis*? You never read the Bible."

"No, and I'm not saying it literally, dummy. But it's like the start of a new world, and this is the Garden of Eden. The world has regenerated, and somehow, we are still here."

"Well, I sure as hell don't get it," he quipped. "It's a bit too much for me. But I do have to say that it is beautiful and peaceful."

They sat until the sun started to sink into the horizon. Chayton walked ahead, back to the truck, as he playfully bounced on the spongy earth. Chenoa followed behind, matching his footprints.

He opened the door to the truck and stepped inside. She opened her door, threw her backpack in first, and smiled at her brother. But then a wince spread across her face, and she fell backward.

"Chenoa?!"

She didn't respond.

He opened his door and ran to the other side of the truck. Chenoa lay on the ground, holding her leg. She said nothing but stared at a creature. Slithering away from her was a shiny black snake with a metallic blue tint.

A shiver rippled through Chayton. He grabbed a shovel from the back of the truck and swung it down on the snake's head. It writhed back and forth before becoming still. He prodded it to make sure it was dead before picking it up. His eyes widened as he recognized the slithering beast.

His voice barely tapped the air. "Chenoa, it's a blue krait."

There was no antivenom for the krait in Bali.

Death was inevitable.

CHAPTER 20

ONE

"CHENOA, STAY AWAKE," Chayton begged as he sped down the road. Dirt from the ground rose beside the truck as he kept his foot down on the pedal.

"Chay, I'm scared," she muttered from the passenger seat.

"Remember what the snake guy, Ron, told us? Venom works differently in different people. So, we're going to the hospital. I have an idea."

"Okay. But if I stop breathing—"

"Just don't. Please, just don't."

He knew the situation. They had learned about the dangers of krait bites for years. Thousands of people died from them every year in India, Sri Lanka, and Indonesia. They were one of the deadliest snakes in the world. Most families around the world kept a reminder of what to do if their kid scraped a knee on the fridge. In Bali, they kept instructions for snake bites.

Chayton's grip tightened on the steering wheel. He wanted to scream but knew he needed to stay composed for his sister. He glanced over at her. Her whole body shook, and her hands were clasped in her lap. *Was she praying?* he wondered. He whispered a prayer to his own unknown god, pleading for him to save his sister.

He sped to the nearest hospital, BIMC, which was only ten minutes away. The lingering issue on his mind was that there were no doctors or staff to help them. They were already dead.

He sped into the main entrance and leaped out of the car. He supported Chenoa as he got her out of the truck. He wasn't sure if she was weak from the bite or the shock. Her whole body still shook, and she shuffled her feet. He pushed the front doors open and paused as a faint hint of disinfectant hit him. He also noted no moldy or mildew odor.

Enough light shone in from the windows to lessen the darkness of the eerie gray lobby. They had been to this hospital before, so he knew there were rooms behind the front desk area. But he needed a flashlight for the windowless back rooms.

"Chay, I'm...not feeling...so great," his sister muttered as they entered a dark room.

"Here. Just lie here," he said as he helped her up onto one of the beds. "I will be right back. I need to find some things."

"Please don't leave me here. It's so dark if you go."

He pulled her flashlight out of his backpack. They had found themselves needing one to explore buildings too many times over the past year; it had become a part of their day packs.

The heavy doors slammed against the walls as he ran from room to room. He knew exactly what he was looking for, so he just prayed they were here. Given the situation over the past years with covid, almost all hospitals carried manual and battery-operated ventilators and endotracheal tubes for intubation. The problem was that there was no power, and the central system running the backup generators had long run out. He found a ventilator and an endotracheal tube in a far supply room.

He ran back to Chenoa. She lay on the bed with her head on a pillow and one leg dangling over the edge. He threw the supplies near her and left once more. He needed power, either a small generator or a portable battery backup system.

A few hallways down, he found a storage closet with battery backup systems. But all of them had no charge, and he had no way of charging them. He frantically searched for a generator, but there was no reason for the hospital to have one in the rooms. He ran his hand through his hair. He had to leave to find one.

He had to leave *her*.

He ran back to her room, almost tripping over himself along the way. He busted through the door and sped to her side. The words spilled out of him. "Chenoa, I need to leave just for a few minutes. I need to go to Ace and get a generator."

"You can't...leave me. Take me with you."

"Ace is just five minutes away. I can drive there, grab a generator, and be back in twenty minutes. It's our only option. There is no power here. *Please*." His voice wavered.

They locked eyes, avoiding the obvious thoughts running in their heads.

"Go," she mumbled. "Please hurry."

He ran to the truck and flew over the curb.

In thirty minutes, he was back with a generator, an extension cord, and a trolley. He loaded the small generator onto the trolley and grabbed one of the diesel containers from the back of the truck. He clumsily pushed everything inside but left the generator just outside the hospital room door, knowing he couldn't run it in the room with the exhaust.

Inside her room, the flashlight lay on the floor, lighting an idyllic rice field scene that was framed as a painting on the opposite wall. He fumbled forward, picked up the light, and shined it on her face. She lay gasping for breath, her face blue.

"Chenoa! Chenoa!" He felt like he had no air himself. "Hold on. I'm back. Please just hold on."

She didn't respond.

His sister was dying.

As he sloshed diesel into the generator, it spilled onto the floor. He desperately pulled the starter cord, yanking it again and again, but he slipped on the slippery gas and fell backward, slamming his head on the tile.

"No, no, no," he said as he got back to his feet. A new pain throbbed through his head. "START you motherfucker!" he yelled, and the engine turned over.

The exhaust needed to be far enough away from the doors. The main lobby had high roofs, but he propped open the front doors to provide added ventilation. He ran the extension cord into Chenoa's room and plugged in the ventilator and a standing lamp. He flicked a switch on the ventilator, and it started a rhythmic, mechanical beat.

Chayton was a trained Wilderness First Aid Responder. He knew CPR, how to mend broken legs, and how to tend burns. But he'd never worked with a ventilator and an endotracheal tube before. Yet this was the only option for a krait bite if she entered respiratory paralysis. They knew more about snake treatments than algebra through their schooling and experience. Snakes were a part of their lives. Yet he had never considered that he would be dealing with a lethal snake bite.

All he remembered was that people died unless they got the right treatment. Even then, they still usually died.

Chenoa's breathing labored, and her face was still blue. He unwrapped the tube and connected it to the ventilator. Her head fell to the side as she blacked out. His heart pounded at the sight, and his hands shook. She lay lifeless on the bed.

He slammed his fist on the bed. "Goddamn it. You are her only hope, so figure this shit out and help her. Figure it out!" he screamed to the empty room.

A picture on the tube's sleeve illustrated how far down the throat it needed to be guided. He tilted her head back and slid the tube further down her throat. His stomach twisted at the sight. He sealed the tube around her mouth with medical tape and flicked the switch once again. The machine began its rhythmic, mechanical breathing.

She still had a pulse, but color was not returning to her face.

He massaged her arms and spoke gently. "Please... Please, Chenoa. You cannot die."

Minutes passed. He knew chest compression wouldn't help since her heart was still beating. Her muscles were just paralyzed from the venom. She couldn't breathe on her own. And the ventilator wasn't working. She wasn't getting enough oxygen.

He reached to remove the tube in her mouth to begin CPR but then stopped. He debated whether to remove the tube and give her mouth-to-mouth or to just leave the tube in. He felt that whatever he chose would kill her.

Her hand slightly quivered.

"Chenoa!" He leaned in closer, massaging her limbs. "Come back. It's me, Chayton. Come on. *Breathe*."

The blue began to fade around her face. She was getting oxygen. He grabbed her hand and placed his head against her palm. He cried.

Color returned to her cheeks. Her pulse steadied.

He waited. Exhausted, he put his head on the bed where his sister lay. He didn't want to fall asleep though. He looked at her as the machine gently raised and lowered her chest.

A vivid memory of them sitting on a park bench in Vancouver came back to him. A light breeze had blown through the maples on a warm summer evening. Red syrupy popsicle juice dripped down the front of her pink dress. He sat next to her, slurping his red popsicle. He wore black sweatpants and a red tie-dye shirt that had a VW logo on the front. He swung his feet back and forth since they couldn't reach the ground. She slowly moved her free hand over to rest on his leg.

He smiled at the memory and then fell asleep.

Something struck Chayton's face. He sat up abruptly to find Chenoa flailing on the table. The generator had stopped. He ran out of the room to find it empty. He filled it—more carefully this time—and restarted the engine.

When he came back into the room, she was grasping at the attachment on her face. It reminded him of the creature from the movie *Alien* that latched onto its host's face, inserted an appendage down their throat, and laid an egg.

He grabbed her shoulders. "It's okay, Chenoa. It's okay. You have a tube in your throat to help you breathe. I'm here."

She let go of the face mask but was disoriented and struggled to steady her breathing. Her eyes darted around, and her body quivered. She reached for her throat, trying to feel for the object in it. She was on the verge of choking but also sensed that the tube was feeding her.

Chayton held her and gently laid her back on the bed. He could tell that her breathing muscles were still paralyzed since her chest had almost no rise or fall. The ventilator was keeping her alive.

"It will be over soon, Chenoa," he muttered. "Just lie still. Then we can go home."

He brushed her head. Her eyes eventually closed, and she fell back to sleep.

The effects of the venom could last from a few hours to a few days.

Chayton had sat with Chenoa for over twenty-four hours. He drank bottled water and ate snacks from the truck. He set up an IV saline drip for her. There was no swelling or bruising where he had inserted the needle, so he knew it was fine.

What if she doesn't wake up? he wondered. *What am I going to do? God—whoever the hell you are—you're going to take my sister from me too? You took my dad's brother. Now, you not only take the entire world but also my sister. What kind of god does something like that? And why would anyone invent a snake that kills people with its bite? What's the point? You suck. You really suck.*

His anger came and went, but his desperation never waned. If she died, then he would follow.

The hospital was quiet except for the ventilator. He lay next to her through the night.

Chenoa died the next morning.

CHAPTER 21

JATI

CHAYTON STOOD IN the middle of the road, staring in the direction of where traffic used to come. He remembered the cars charging down the highway, only to stop ahead as the traffic bottlenecked.

Running to stand still. His dad used to play a song with that line in it. People were busy or acting busy, rushing to get somewhere that they either didn't need to be or didn't want to be. A race to nowhere, irrelevant and meaningless.

Nietzsche, he thought. *Didn't he say that life was meaningless? Yeah, but there were a lot more people around then. Now, everyone's gone. Meaningless.*

The sun pounded on the tar and the motionless boy who now sat on the road. A small community of chimps wandered down the street, giving a wide berth to the statuesque being. A curious baby walked over to Chayton and sat next to him. The mother turned toward her baby. She reached for him to leave, seeming unsure of the creature sitting on the road. But then she sat next to the boy with the baby chimp sitting between the two.

The rest of the chimps halted their progress and sat, waiting. The baby gently placed his hand on the boy's knee and quietly maneuvered into the boy's lap. Chayton looked down at the baby and placed his hand face up. The baby placed his hand atop his. The mother slid over next to the boy.

They all sat. Quiet. Considering. Wondering.

Chayton lay back on the burning pavement. He liked the pain. He wanted the sun to desecrate his body, and then the wind could disperse him. The sun punished him, soothing him.

He drifted off to sleep and dreamed.

Below him, a boy sat in the middle of a road. A chimp and her baby sat next to him. The boy looked up toward him yet made no acknowledgment. He recognized the boy on the ground. But he couldn't place him.

He floated upward. The details of the world below blurred as he rose. An island, vast and green, opened underneath him. He knew the island, but he couldn't place it. Yet the island became a verdant dot next to a string of other islands that contrasted against a deep blue ocean. Blue and green.

The world disappeared below. He expanded. He felt nothing and everything. He was here and there.

Chenoa.

He knew that name.

Chenoa?

"Chenoa?" the sleepy boy whispered.

The mother chimp jumped as the boy spoke, cradled her baby under her belly, and rejoined the other chimps. Chayton rolled up to a seating position and watched as they moved southward down the road.

He stood and turned back toward the hospital but then stopped. He was soulless. Empty. He turned from the hospital and followed the chimps instead.

Haze hovered over the pavement. His feet burned from the heat, bearing through his soles. He didn't notice the chimps leaving the road and moving into the jungle. The baby looked back at Chayton, but he stared blankly ahead.

He stopped in the middle of the road. He knew he couldn't just abandon her body. He also knew he didn't have the strength to see her again. He imagined her lifeless form and shook his head.

His dad had described the anguish he had felt from his brother's death. His dad didn't want to remember his brother as an inanimate corpse but as the vibrant being he once was.

Chayton turned back to the hospital.

He would hold some ceremony for her, and that would be his last act for this world. At least then he would know if there was life after death. He would either be with Mom and Dad and Chenoa, or he wouldn't. If the latter, then so be it.

A shadow came across his path. He looked up and shielded his eyes from the sun.

Four herons flew overhead.

The generator rumbled in the hospital lobby, creating a faint cloud of blue smoke that hovered near the ceiling. Chayton had no concept of how long he had been gone. The room stood like a vast tomb. Dust mites flitted in the light.

He stopped and winced, cringing at the thought of pulling the tube out of Chenoa's mouth and carrying her body out to the truck. *Will I put her in the front next to me? Or will I lay her in the back? Do I need to protect her head?*

He decided to bring her home and bury her under the Bodhi tree. Their dad had buried Jasper, a sparrow that had struck the window in their prior villa and was taken for dead, there. Chenoa had nursed it back to health, and it lived for a few days. Jasper would rest on her belly as she slept or read. The bird was her friend. When it had died, she was devastated. Their dad had suggested they bury it at their new Villa Jati under the Bodhi tree. She had liked the idea.

His dad had always wanted to bring some of his brother's and dad's ashes back to Bali and spread them under the tree. Chayton knew that would never happen now, but there was a comfort in the fact her body would be cared for by the trees, one which their mom and dad had planted and sat under.

He recalled her middle name: Jati. The namesake of their dad's brother. Jati, the cycle of life and death.

Birth. Life. Death. That's all there is to this world, he thought.

He pushed open the door to her room and waited for his eyes to adjust. The lamp cast its glow onto the floor and on a part of the table where she lay. He shuffled forward and stood over her body. He had covered her with a white blanket that he had found in the closet before he left. Her little body appeared as a thin outline under the covers. Tears streamed down his face as he pulled back the blanket.

"Chayton."

The bed lay empty. He must've been imagining things.

"Chay?"

He turned toward the voice.

Chenoa sat on the neighboring bed. She appeared ghostly in the reflected light from the lamp.

He moved toward her and placed his hands on her face. "Chenoa?"

"Hi, Chay."

He sat next to his sister, observing her. She appeared weak. She still had an empty IV bag attached to her arm, which dangled from the mobile bedside hanger. He gently removed the needle, watching as a droplet of blood dripped down her arm from where the needle had been. He wiped her arm with the bedsheet but kept his hand near her. He was cautious since she appeared so fragile. The thought of speaking or moving her frightened him.

So, they sat for a very long time.

"Is there any water?" she eventually asked.

He somewhat reluctantly ran to the truck and grabbed the backpack with water and some fruit. He didn't want this all to be a dream. He pushed open the doors to her room, expecting her to not be sitting on the bed.

But she was.

He opened the backpack and handed her a bottle. "Here you go. Just drink a little. Are you hungry?"

"Maybe."

He opened a banana and handed it to her. She nibbled at the end before taking larger bites and methodically chewing.

"Chenoa? How?" he asked eventually.

She wasn't sure how to respond, so she kept eating and drinking for a few minutes.

"I had strange dreams, Chay," she admitted after a while. "You, Mom, and Dad were there. You would come and go, but I'm not sure why. Then I started choking. I tried to sit up but couldn't move and reached for my mouth. I found the tube and tried to scream. I just ripped at it, and my lungs and throat burned. I gagged and heaved. I had no idea what was happening, and you were gone."

"I'm so sorry," he said. "I should have been here."

"Then I remembered where I was and what had happened. I know you had talked to me about the tube before I passed out. I remembered."

"When did you wake up? How long have you been here?"

"I don't know."

She cried softly at first but then sobbed. He held her, and they shook uncontrollably as they wept. He pulled her tight to his chest and rested his chin on her head.

He cared for her until color came back to her face, and her energy returned. He then walked her out to the truck and placed her in the front seat. He grimaced, recalling his earlier image of placing her dead body into the car. He reached across to put on her seat belt.

"Chay, I don't need a seat belt," she said.

"Please just wear it."

He drove home slowly, constantly looking over in her direction to check on her. On edge, he knew it was the adrenaline surging through his body, a natural stimulant to ensure he got her home safely.

A darkness lingered in his chest. But there was also light. The light grew as he drove. He admired the sky and the cumulus clouds that formed above. The trees waved through a breeze that came off the ocean. A pride of lions rested atop a grassy hill, while a herd of elephants fed alongside a pack of deer.

Chayton pulled the truck over and wailed. He struggled to catch his breath, and he hugged himself, leaning his head on the steering wheel.

Chenoa turned and put her hand on his shoulder. "What's the matter, Chay? I'm okay. We're okay."

He looked at her and continued to weep. "I left you. I thought you were dead. What if I had left you there alone, Chenoa? I thought you were gone. I didn't want to live."

"But you came back. You came back." She gave him a hug. "Drive. We are going to be all right, Chay."

He looked over, and she had fallen asleep.

Darkness dissipated. And light shone.

Hope had returned.

CHAPTER 22

HEALING

A DEEP MIST floated up through the valley, driven by a northern breeze. The thick, moist air foretold an impending storm. A monkey call pierced the silence.

Chayton stood rigid with his arms crossed, staring at the foggy apparition. He couldn't recall such a fog. The temperatures had shifted over the past many months, creating cooler mornings and evenings and offering the island a reprieve from the tropical midday heat.

A large bird emerged from the mist and perched itself on a frangipani tree. It had a black throat and a cream-colored cap with a golden-brown plume that stretched over more than half of its body. A bird of paradise. It tilted its head, observing the boy who stood along the deck. It hopped from its perch, landed along the pool's edge, and drank.

He remembered his dad's love of the bird of paradise flower. His dad loved the bright red and yellow firmly structured flower as it bent over in the shape of a bird's head. They had planted the flowers all about the property. They were framed in the kitchen window and through all the bedrooms at the end of the long hallway. He would occasionally cut some and place them in vases for their mom.

Chayton pursed his lips and forced his eyes shut, pushing away the painful memories. His parents were gone, and he didn't have the time or the strength to deal with a sentimental parental film reel.

Chenoa had slept for most of the last two days. He would check on her, sometimes getting close enough to ensure she was breathing without disturbing her. He recalled hearing parents say that they did the same with their newborns, hovering over their children while confirming air continued to move in and out. He kept lemon water and fruit next to her bed stand. Banana peels and empty passion fruits littered the stand and the floor, so he knew she was eating something.

Kubi cuddled next to her, and Kuma rested on the floor. They always stayed with her, only coming out to eat or to go to the bathroom. Machi followed Chayton wherever he went, prancing a few feet behind and wagging her tail.

"Thank you, girl." He stopped and hugged her. "I don't know how, but you dogs seem to get something that us humans don't understand. Mom understood you the best. Humans could have learned a lot from you pooches."

He remembered an article his dad had written for Medium called "My Wife is a Dog." It was a self-deprecating piece about his cleanliness and frustrations with the dogs, but it was mostly about how Mom loved animals so much. He had said that whenever he looked into the dog's eyes, he saw her.

Chayton cradled Machi's face and looked deeply into her eyes. "Mom?" he asked.

She didn't move but then blinked and licked his mouth.

"Ew, girl." He patted her head and smiled.

He had restarted the generator, so he turned on the lights around the home to bring some comfort. After plugging his phone into the Sony music player, he found his dad's favorites playlist. He hit shuffle, and Eddie Vedder's gravelly voice came through singing "Hard Sun." A smile crossed his lips. Dad had always talked about this song, playing it way too often as they sat around the dinner table.

"I love this song," his dad had said. "This was from that movie *Into the Wild*, where the boy leaves everything—"

"Yeah, Dad. You've told us," Chayton had said, smirking.

"And the ending? Did I mention that?"

"Yes," Chenoa had responded. "Happiness needs to be shared."

Their dad had smiled, nodding. "That's right. Happiness needs to be shared."

The song ended, and Chayton put it on repeat, letting it run on a continuous loop. "There you are, Dad. I love it too."

"Hey, Chay."

Chayton turned from where he sat on the deck in front of the pool, surprised to see his sister. She looked weak, moving slowly with her arms hugging her chest.

"How are you feeling?" he asked.

"I dreamed a lot. Not all good dreams. Some were dark."

"Me too. Maybe we were in the same dreams," he said. "Are you hungry?"

"Yes. And thirsty."

He made her a plate of grilled chicken and vegetables with some fruit, and he opened a fresh coconut. "Here you go. And drink this. It's all you need and has electrolytes," he offered, quoting their mom.

A mother and a baby deer had jumped the fence onto their property and were feeding on the grassy patches between the deck and the pool. They occasionally raised their heads to observe the two children sitting on the deck.

The dogs, though still patrolling the property and barking at nighttime noises, no longer chased the animal intruders that frequented their yard, except for rats and, thankfully, snakes. But those were rare. Perhaps with no more humans, they moved back to their natural habitats. The occasional found snake was scooped up and tossed over the wall. The children still refused to kill any snake, even if it was poisonous.

Chayton had kept the generator running since it gave Chenoa comfort to have music playing and lights on at night, but he knew that the diesel was running low. "Chenoa, I need to find some more diesel for the generator. Do you want to stay here?"

"No," she responded quickly. "Can I come with you? I feel okay." She rubbed where the snake had bitten her leg. All that remained were two dots and a red irritation around the wound.

He knew she didn't want to be alone. He didn't want to leave her alone either.

They packed the truck with empty diesel tanks and supplies for the day. They still carried guns with them just in case. The dogs bounced around them, expressing their desire to go along. Piki seemed content to stay as he lay on the back porch, so they leashed the other three dogs to the truck bed sockets and headed out.

They filled the containers at a gas station just outside of Ubud. An abandoned petrol truck continued to provide the supply they needed. Yet when they'd drive away each time, they wondered when the tank would run dry.

Chayton touched the *Junglo* sticker along the driver's door, recalling his partners who had not only worked with him but had mentored him throughout his life. The reminders of their past life diminished each day as nature continued its reclamation. Outside of a few buildings, temples, vehicles, and telephone poles, there was little left to show humanity's history. Even the phone and power cables had mostly fallen to the ground and been eaten by the earth. He didn't miss the signs and advertisements that had littered the roads though. All of that was junk in his mind. He only wished his family and friends were still around.

"Chay, let's go," his sister called from inside the truck. "What are you doing?"

"Just thinking and remembering."

They decided to drive down south to Pererenan to head to the beach. Pererenan had been their home for two months before they had moved into their current home. They had lived with their friends and their two sons in one of their spare traditional home rentals.

Chenoa considered the world as it passed by the window. Bali was gone. Culture and tradition meant nothing, never to be recollected or passed on. Perhaps

Shiva and Saraswati continued to exist, along with the other deities from different religions. Did they now sit together in a long hall, reflecting on their failed experiments with humankind? Was the demise their doing? Or was the great hall empty, only a fictional relic created by humans to address their needs and unanswerable questions? She smiled and shook her head as she envisioned a roomful of divine beings.

God is there, she thought as she looked at the trees and the animals along the roadway. *God has always been there. She just wasn't what most people thought she was. And she was never enough.*

"Never enough," she said aloud.

"What was that, Chenoa?" her brother asked.

"Nothing. Just thinking about what we had. Or thought we had."

They stopped where the road ended. The parking lot was gone as were the warungs and the small hotels that had sat back from the beach. There were no grassy plots for people to sit on. The ocean now reached up to the end of the road. Sandy beaches returned to where they had been years before. False breakwaters and barriers to keep out the oceanic world had crumbled. The pounding surf had washed away human constructions.

Pererenan sat between two rivers that flowed into the Indian Ocean. The usually polluted rivers now ran clear and free of any plastic.

The siblings grabbed their packs and let the dogs out of the truck. They walked westward along the more naturally formed and extended beach.

Chayton took off his shirt and walked out into the flowing estuary. Crustaceans filled the riverbed. Schools of small fish parted in front of him when he moved through the water. He fell back, scrunching his face as he went under since he still was not wholly convinced the water was healthy. But then he let the pure water flow into his mouth. Like the river water near their home, this water was clean and succulent.

He drank, shaking his head in complete disbelief. "Come on in, Chenoa. It's not so fast, and it's refreshing."

She took off her pants and shirt, only leaving her undergarments. She was still a bit careful, but the brisk water soothed her body. "Oh, Chayton. This is so nice."

Kuma, Machi, and Kubi joined them in the water. They raced in and out of the river, attempting to leap the width as they chased each other.

The water healed all of them. And reassured them. Seeing how the southern river was clean at this point made it clear to the children that the island had fully cleansed itself of its poisons.

In the warm midday sun, they sat on the sand. The dogs continued to chase each other up and down the beach. They knew their mom would have been so happy to witness this with the dogs and the children.

Chayton lay back in the sand and fell asleep. Chenoa noticed his pronounced chin and broad shoulders were just like their dad's. For a moment, she thought she was looking at their dad. Chay wasn't a little boy anymore. And the past two years had hardened him. He was still the jokester she knew, but the death and destruction and constant trials had toughened him both physically and mentally. How could it not have? She felt much the same about herself. She saw her mom looking back at her in the mirror each morning.

She left him lying in the sand since she knew he was exhausted. She slipped on her pants and headed down the beach. The warm sand felt good against her feet. She walked along the edge to where the waves reached. The water washed away her footsteps as she walked. Sand flicked in the air off to her right. A baby turtle had pushed its way out from its nest and instinctively moved toward the water.

She considered helping it to the water but hesitated. "You don't need my help, do you little fella?"

The turtle pushed itself along with its flippers, erratic in its movements. It made its way to the water and slid into the surf. Something tickled her foot, and she jumped. Another baby turtle had crawled over her foot and now lay on its back, flapping its flippers.

"Oh!" She gently turned it onto its belly. "There you go, little one."

It scooted toward the water. A trail of turtles came out of the nest, reminding her of a Disney parade. She sat in the sand and counted them as they passed.

"...thirty-two, thirty-three, and thirty-four. There sure are a lot of you."

Thirty-four made its way into the water, and she stood to leave. Another flick of sand came from the nest. Followed by more sprays of sand. A smaller turtle struggled to get out of the nest. The others had left a large depression in the sand, and the wall was too steep for it to crawl out. She dug a gradual incline from the nest's edge for about one meter. The turtle followed the trench out and shuffled toward the water.

But unlike the other turtles, this one stopped at the water's edge and waited.

"Come on. You can do it," she coaxed.

The baby stayed put.

She walked up next to it and sat on the sand. The water soaked her pants. "You don't want to go, do you? I get it. That ocean looks kind of scary to me as well at times."

They didn't move for a few minutes. Then she stood and walked into the water. She let it get to her shins before stopping and waiting. The baby turtle pushed forward with its fins. A small wave pushed it back, but it scampered forward and swam by her feet. She watched it disappear into the crystal blue water.

"Where were you?" Chayton asked as he sat up. He was a bit red from lying in the sun, and sand dripped off his back.

"I was just walking and helping some little friends."

The siblings finished their drinks and food as the sun started to set on the horizon. The dogs had worn themselves out by now and lay sprawled out in the sand around them. Kubi eyed a crab scrambling across the sand but was too tired to chase it. Afterward, they gathered their belongings and made their way back to the truck. Kuma and Machi jumped into the truck bed, and they leashed them to the fasteners. But Kubi stood, facing the beach and barking.

"Come on, boy," Chenoa called. "Let's go. The crab will still be here when we come back."

He stood firm, so she went to get him.

"Come on. Let's go. You are always barking at something." She looked down at the beach but saw nothing. "There is nothing there, Kubi." She tied him up in the back of the truck, and he strained against the leash.

"He doesn't want to leave," Chayton said. "He's having fun."

They drove back home, talking and laughing the entire way, while Kubi intently watched the horizon.

A blurry, dark shape appeared where the water met the sky.

CHAPTER 23

LAST BREATH

THE LIZARD HID just out of reach of Kubi's snout. The dog had been chasing the terrified reptile through the banana trees that lined the wall. Machi dug next to Chayton as he created rows of raised garden beds.

He and his sister were planting vegetables in the garden since the rainy season had come to an end. Tropical downpours could break new sprouts that were pushing up out of the ground. Chenoa pushed seeds of kale, onions, eggplant, corn, and tomatoes into the dark fertile soil. The garden already provided mango, papaya, avocado, lemons, and pineapple. He cut open a pineapple and handed her a dripping slice. He cut himself a mango.

Their yards had been converted into gardens. The only lawn remaining was the sliver between the porch and the pool. They had planted pineapples along the eastern slope below the pool. Coconuts grew in the neighboring yards. New plants grew and flourished as the seeds spread from the fallen fruit.

Animals also fed on the food, passing the seeds in their drops as nature intended. Animals and humans no longer competed. Food wasn't wasted. No animal was killed without cause.

The world was back in balance.

Chenoa uprooted a selection of vines and small plants to place into bottles with water for her room. Her room was now a greenery with creepers drooping down walls and green shoots filling nooks and crannies. Her favorite place was her loft, where she could quietly sit with no distractions. Her crystals sat on the table along with some fragrant candles. The candles' scents would remind her of different times: Mother's Day, Christmas, and Thanksgiving. They sat within a ring of pottery that the family had all made at a class one Christmas. The loft was her sanctuary, and she felt the most connected to her mom and dad there.

She also was reading *The Lord of the Rings*. It was enjoyable but not her favorite. Yet it was her dad's favorite book, so she read it, believing he was reading it with her. She also would recall her dreamy discussion with her mom about her loft being her hobbit hole, her safe place.

Her and Chayton planted the seeds and watered them. They then went back to the house with baskets of fruits and vegetables. Shopping was significantly easier than before.

He decided to make a feast that evening. So, he collected a few chickens along with some eggs. He had perfected mango and rice pudding, which was her favorite.

"The meal is delicious, Chay," she said at dinner. "And the dogs are happy with their chickens."

As he stepped out near the pool to give Machi another chicken leg, he noticed an orange movement near the deck. He walked over with Kuma following behind him.

Clumsily stepping up over the deck edge, a small tiger cub appeared. Kuma growled, but he told her to stop. Just behind the cub rose an enormous tiger, who shook her head to the side and growled.

"Tigger!" he yelled. He moved forward, while Kuma observed the cub and nuzzled it with her snout. "Chenoa! Look who's here!"

She came over and yelled with delight. "Tigger! Come here, girl." She turned to the cub playing with her pant leg. "Oh my gosh. You are so cute!" She rolled onto the ground with the cub as the mother nudged Chayton's hand for the chicken.

He willingly offered up the chicken leg. "If there is a baby, that means there is a daddy around somewhere, Chenoa," he said. "So, keep an eye out."

"I'm just glad she found a partner to have a baby with. Oh, I want to keep this one!"

He fetched two more chickens and fed them to the tigers. He wondered why Tigger never took the chickens from their coop. Maybe she understood that they were for the children. And with all the deer roaming the island, maybe she didn't need to take their food.

The dogs and Tigger lazed on the grass. The siblings sat on the porch as the sun settled over the hills.

"Thanks, Chay," Chenoa said after a moment. The tiger cub lay on its back at her feet, swatting at the palm leaf she dangled in front of her.

"No problem, Chenoa. I was happy to make you a meal."

"Not just for the meal...but for everything." She turned to face him. "We've been through so much, and if I was alone, and that snake bit me, then I'd be dead."

"Don't talk about it, Chenoa. We are fine, and we are okay." He smiled and gently tapped her shoulder with his fist.

"I know. But thank you." The cub had fallen asleep between her feet. She brushed its soft fur and whispered, "Thank you."

They nibbled on their pudding and drank coconut water. Dusk brought the transition to night, and bats darted above the pond.

"Chenoa, do you think it's fine that I actually feel happy? I mean, I miss everyone, but we get to see this." He waved his hand across the valley in front of them.

"Of course. I wish Mom and Dad were back, but I do wake up each day now and smile that you are here along with the dogs and all of our new animal friends. It's different. Okay. It's *really* different, and I miss having more people around. But I never could have imagined how beautiful and perfect the world could have been. It's sad that it required all that bad to happen to see this."

"You're right. It is pretty amazing. It doesn't just look different; it feels different. I can feel the world *breathing*, Chenoa. Maybe we were choking the world."

A faint breeze pushed through the valley, and the trees swayed in an undulating rhythm.

"Oh yeah," she agreed. "We were choking it. I know this sounds weird, but I think I can hear it talking to me. Not with words but something else. I know that's silly though."

"No, I feel it too. I just don't think we were listening very well before. People stopped listening to each other, and we all stopped listening to the earth."

The siblings listened to the quieting valley as they ate, content and happy for the first time in years. Twinkling stars—tiny beacons of hope—blanketed the sky.

The world was healing. The trees inhaled and exhaled. The children exhaled.

A shadow passed in front of the driveway's gate, and a bloodshot eye peered in through the opening. A hand fumbled to slide the latch. The figure slid the gate open, trying to not break the evening's stillness.

She stood still for a moment, watching and listening, before reaching for a knife that hung off her belt by her side. The presence shuffled forward, toward the villa. Her left leg dragged behind her, and her body curved. Blood scabbed on a bruised arm.

A coucal called into the night.

Since the generator had run out of fuel, the villa was in darkness. The children had already gone to bed, leaving all the dogs lounging near the pool under the moonlit evening. They were not aware of the figure as she tested the doors before finding one that the children had forgotten to lock. A full moon lit the room, showing her the furniture to step around. But instead, she stood still for a long time, turning her head and looking.

Kubi lifted his head, sensing movement from within the home. His breath steamed the window as he strained to see inside, but the moon's reflection on the glass clouded his view. He ran down the porch and to the entry door outside the children's rooms.

The figure now stood in front of Chayton's room. She slid his door open and stepped inside.

Kubi barked and slammed against the locked door. The other dogs joined in, scratching at the door to get inside.

Chayton abruptly sat up in his bed and saw a silhouette framed in the doorway. He reached for his bedside light and switched it on, but nothing happened. There was no power. He pushed himself to the far side of his bed to reach for his knife. "Get out of here!" he screamed. "Get out of here!"

The figure stood still. She whimpered and then cried.

He almost grabbed his knife but paused at the figure's demeanor. "Who are you?" He fumbled for a flashlight instead and shined it toward the doorway.

A face appeared: bloodied, exhausted, and dirty.

Chenoa stormed down the hallway with a baseball bat in hand. She approached with the bat raised above her head as the dogs continued to slam against the outside door. But she stopped when the figure's face turned toward her. A familiar face. One she thought she'd never see again.

"Mom?"

CHAPTER 24

AFTER

THEY CRIED. HUGGED. Cried some more.

The three collapsed onto the floor in fumbling desperation. Their mom held each of their faces and kissed them. She trembled with delight and anxiety that this might stop. That they might disappear.

Chenoa opened the back door to let the dogs in. They swarmed Jo and licked her whole face. Chayton and Chenoa laughed beside them. It was a huddled pile of love on the hallway floor. Years of despair flooding out. They said little to each other.

But Chayton knew someone had to ask. "Where's Dad?"

Their mom looked at them as tears welled up in her eyes. "He's...he's gone."

The kids sat back and listened to their mom tell her story.

"The skies had turned cloudy so quickly," Jo said. "The event organizers were concerned about a tropical storm. But we quickly saw that it wasn't a storm. The darkness came from the west, over the swimmers who were heading to the island. All I could think about was your Dad. I ran to find a boat. All the captains were on their radios, listening to the panic coming in over their speakers. One told me that something was wrong and that the boats were returning.

"The dark cloud kept coming, and as it got closer to the shore, people started coughing. I ran. I was so scared, and I couldn't get to him." Her voice cracked, and her lips quivered.

"People screamed and ran," she continued. "I rushed into a hotel lobby that was near the event. Some people came through the entrance, retching and then collapsing. I thought it was some kind of poison attack.

"A lady dressed in a hotel uniform yelled at a group of us to follow, but everyone else ran away. She took me down to a lower level and locked us in a staff room. We got online and saw the news. I tried to call both of you, but nothing was getting through."

She grabbed her head and cried. The kids put their arms around her.

"It's okay, Mom. You don't need to tell us now," Chenoa soothed.

"No. You need to know," she said, wiping tears away with the back of her hand. "We stayed there for a day. I wanted to go out and see if he had come back, but from what we had read online, I knew Chris was dead. The next day, we came out to find bodies strewn all over the streets. Everyone was gone. *Everyone*. Over the next few weeks, we found a few people who had survived. I went to the beach every day to see if your dad would come home.

"Most of the people with us were Australian, but a few had traveled there for the race. We trekked to Melbourne and Sydney by car and truck. The situation was the same. Just a handful of survivors. Some of us eventually decided that we needed to try and come back to Bali. We found a boat in Darwin and someone to captain it for us. Five of us made the journey here."

She stopped for a moment, not wanting to recall what had happened next. "There was a mom and a dad and a young boy. Maybe six. The boy died one evening. The parents had lost the only person who mattered to them. We held a ceremony since we knew we couldn't keep the body on the boat. We wrapped the little boy in a blue-green linen and gently put him into the water.

"As we watched his body float away in the current, a fin appeared, and a splash washed over the boy. The father grabbed the mom and held her tight. His expression was blank. Emotionless. But that evening, there was a splash. The mom had jumped overboard. The father ran to the edge and jumped in after her.

"We tried to find them, but the darkness and the current prevented it. We also still had half of our trip to make and needed our fuel. A note had been left on the table below. It simply read ENOUGH.'

"It was just me and the captain then. He told me that he had a wife and two kids who had died in the event. We came to shore in Sanur. I grabbed my small pack with some supplies and waded ashore. Then the engine started, and the boat backed away. He raised his hand toward me and smiled.

"I raised my hand in return, smiled back at him, and mouthed the words *thank you*. He tipped his head toward me and drove the boat away. He had done his last job as a captain."

They sat still for a long time, just a mother and her children processing what she had shared. She eventually broke the silence.

"So, tell me what had happened here," their mom said.

The children told their tale, interrupting each other. Chayton started to tell the river story, but Chenoa gently shook her head. It wasn't time. They left the river, the scuba diving, and the snake bite incidents for another day. Their mom watched them, smiling in disbelief.

"Is there anyone else on the island?" their mom asked.

"There were two people," Chayton said. "But they weren't good people. Tigger took care of them."

"Tigger?"

"Our tiger."

Their mom paused for a moment. "You...you have a tiger?"

"Two now actually. And an elephant."

Jo looked at both of her children. She realized they were no longer kids but young adults. Their bodies had drastically changed over the past two years: muscular and lean. And she heard the change in their now knowing and wise voices.

Chenoa looked at the cuts and scrapes along her mom's face and body. A poorly healed scar ran down her upper arm. She wanted to ask her mom what had happened but refrained. Her mom's body told a story of fighting and struggling to get back to her children.

She brushed a few strands of hair out of her mom's eyes. "I'm so sorry, Mom." She hugged her, holding her tight.

Chayton put his arm around Kuma and pulled her close.

Chenoa helped her mom shower. Blood and dirt circled into the drain. Her mom sat on the floor as she brushed her hair. Her mom had brushed her hair so many times over the years. It was a mother-daughter ritual to them. But now the roles had reversed.

She had been wearing her mom's clothes, just as Chayton had been wearing his dad's. So, she took some clothes out of her closet and gave them back to her mom. After her mom had showered and dressed in clean clothes, Chenoa felt her mom was back. Finally back. She snuggled into her, happy that the journey smell was gone. She smelled like Mom again.

They ate fish and fruit on the porch, while the dogs lounged on the deck, gnawing on raw chicken. They spoke endlessly about their experiences since they had last seen each other. Chenoa told their mom everything that had happened. Their mom didn't like hearing it all, but she listened and marveled at them.

"I miss him," Chenoa said.

"I'm so sorry I couldn't find him," Mom cried. She turned to Chayton and cupped his face in her hands. "You look just like him though, Chay. It is astonishing."

"That makes me happy, Mom," he responded with a glimmer in his eyes.

She smiled. "And you look like someone else I know, Chenoa."

The sun fell over the back of the house and cast its shadow across the pool. A flock of herons headed east above them. A coucal's call echoed through the valley. In front of them, a blue butterfly landed on the table and gently waved its wings.

"It's *amazing*," Chayton said, smiling.

EPILOGUE

HOPE

WAVES WASHED AGAINST the shore as the evening sun set the sky ablaze. A family of quokka—small brown mammals about the size of a domestic cat and with a bear-like face—played along the beach. An osprey shot from the sky with its talons extended. The quokkas darted into the safety of the bush behind them. The bird circled twice before continuing its search along the shore.

A man sat at the edge of the shore break, watching the osprey hunt. The bird glanced toward him and hovered for a moment before diving toward the surf. The water exploded as it briefly submerged. It then reappeared and flew away with its silvery catch.

The man stared across the channel crossing. He closed his eyes, muttering words for the wind to carry. Turning his ear, he listened for a response. None ever came. Still, he repeated it each day.

He stood and brushed sand off his tattered jeans. His blue, threadbare T-shirt flapped in the offshore wind. He pointlessly rubbed at a spot on his shirt and then flat-tened it downward in an effort to remove the wrinkles. He knew it was meaningless, but he did it anyway.

From down the beach, another man called to him. A group of men, women, and children circled a roaring fire. They warmly motioned for him to come. He waved back and smiled. They knew he would join them eventually. He'd greet everyone and sit quietly, entering the conver-sation in his own time.

It was his daily ritual as the sun gave way to the stars after all.

He turned back toward the ocean as a humpback whale rolled and waved its pectoral fin, reflecting orange across the water in the fading light.

The man placed his hands on his heart and smiled.

"Amazing."

THE END

ACKNOWLEDGMENTS

I ORIGINALLY WROTE *Butterfly* for my children and to honor my brother, but I wrote it without ever telling my family. Then others suggested that I publish it.

My book is a love letter to my children. It is very personal and outside of the volcanic event, is based on fact. It is admittedly unusual. And there was much sensitivity around the writing as I used my family as the characters. My wife and children did read and comment before it was published. I made a number of edits based on their feedback.

My intention was to share my thoughts on life without boring my kids to death. I guess I failed miserably in one way since I knocked them off a few times throughout the novel. But I tried to put my feelings into a format that they would enjoy. I also wanted to create a context that encouraged them to appreciate each other and what they have in life. The loss of my brother was devastating.

Sometimes it is only through loss that we appreciate what we have.

I had wanted to write a novel for years, so I signed up for David Wheeler's online writing course with Coursera. I thought writing it was going to be the hard part. How little I knew about this whole writing process.

Robin LeeAnn from Reedsy walked me through the three-month editing process. Sam Pearce from SWATT Books managed the entire art, design, formatting, publishing, and distribution process for me. They were both professional, patient, and very kind to me throughout the project.

I worked on much of my book through my writer's club in Bali, Indonesia. Though I did the writing secretly, everyone in the writing group knew of my journey. They didn't realize how much they had helped me.

Some may wonder why I'm selling the book since I only wrote it for my kids. It is a good question. I did consider giving it away for free, but there is a cost to publishing and printing a book. There is also a more important issue.

One theme of the book is about the regeneration of the world. There are a few groups who are working to make the world a better place that are close to my heart. I will give a portion of the profits to the following groups: Women's Earth Alliance (womensearthalliance. org), Junglo (junglo.org), Earth Company (earthcompany. info), and Astungkara Way (astungkaraway.com). These groups are empowering women, planting native forests, supporting social projects, and bringing regenerative and organic farming back to Bali. I wish everyone was doing the work of these organizations.

As a final note, not once did I question writing my novel until one day in the publishing process, I stopped to ask myself: *what if people don't like it?* This was so odd to me, and for a few weeks, the question played around in my head.

Then I remembered my own advice that I gave to Chayton and Chenoa: just be yourself and do your best.

I am happy with what I have done. I hope you enjoyed it.

Thank you.

Amazing. 🦋

Made in the USA
Las Vegas, NV
28 July 2023

75348426R00136